CONTAGION
TO THIS
WORLD

CONTAGION TO THIS WORLD

A PARALLEL UNIVERSE STORY

Julie McCulloch Burton

CONTAGION TO THIS WORLD
A PARALLEL UNIVERSE STORY

iUniverse books may be ordered through booksellers or by contacting:

iUniverse
1663 Liberty Drive
Bloomington, IN 47403
www.iuniverse.com
1-800-Authors (1-800-288-4677)

ISBN: 978-1-5320-3008-6 (sc)
ISBN: 978-1-5320-3009-3 (hc)
ISBN: 978-1-5320-3007-9 (e)

Library of Congress Control Number: 2017912710

Print information available on the last page.

iUniverse rev. date: 11/20/2017

You are not going to like this book.

PARALLEL UNIVERSE

Also called an alternative universe, or a multiverse, a parallel universe is a separate universe or world that coexists with our known universe but is very different from it.

(Dictionary.com)

Part I
A PRIORI

Part II
A POSTERIORI

Part III
A PRIORI

PART I

A PRIORI

CHAPTER 1

HEAT RISES

Leaving Earth with a burst of speed and a trail of dark exhaust, the Saturnian Space Agency performed what had become routine: Eight people were on their way to relieve the entire crew of a low-Earth orbit space research station. Unbeknownst to the agency's flight surgeons or to the crew itself, a hypervirulent bacterium had hitched a ride. For one week, both crews mingled sharing food, toilets and sleeping quarters, and then the crew that had been relieved flew home for the usual six month break.

This time, though, they would not be returning to the space station: A superbug as dangerous as the long-feared MRSA (methicillin-resistant *Staphylococcus aureus*) had arrived with a healthy-looking crewmember. Zander, our very own Typhoid Mary, brought with her death in the form of a pan-resistant superinfection *Salmonella typhi*, the bacterium that causes typhoid fever.

"…I've read your reports. You've briefed me on-station. I relieve you," Zander stated formally.

"I stand relieved," Echo spoke just as formally but was slouched in a chair, and then she clicked-off comms to Earth.

"Now," she whooped, "let's get this party started. Feed me Seymour."

The on-coming team cooked the first meal, so Zander headed for the galley. This would be the first time (or the last time) in six months that this crew would be getting fresh fruits and veggies not grown on-site, along with fresh meat and milk, so this event had evolved into a traditional feast. Breakfast the following day would be French toast made with precious real eggs, fresh sourdough bread and bananas that were within their three-minute window of being an edible yellow.

"Are they still going at it?" someone asked.

"Yep," Feis shrugged, "their loss. More food for us. Ohhh, and drink! Pass that over here, will ya?"

"Paying their dues at the Skyle-High Club?"

"Travis, you say that every time, and it's still not funny."

"It was once, and will be again. I'll give it six months."

When both teams were assembled later that evening, it was time for some shop-talk. Zander, experienced with the routine of running this station, known as the *Oasis*, spoke with ease to the group, handing out duties that would aid with the staffing turn-over.

With a standing crew of eight, only three maintained the *Oasis*. The other five were scientists and engineers tasked with designing a better way to live for extended periods of time in space. The lines were blurred when an engineer worked on the station's oxygen generator or a scientist tested storing packaged freeze-dried food outside strapped to the hull of the space station rather than in the proper storage compartment near the galley. The botanist maintained the greenhouse, but the crew must keep the water, light and air mixture steady and continuous.

Whatever their area of expertise might be, they were all shipmates, and they all must work together. One of the earliest lessons learned was that no matter how brilliant someone was, if one didn't get along well with others, then one didn't belong on the station. "Leave your ego on the launch pad," was beaten into them endlessly during training. Added to that was, "Annoying habits will keep you grounded." Peer review was as important as any instruction or medical test.

It would be extremely close quarters for a week. With only eight bunks, the sixteen people now on-station would sleep in shifts, hot-racking: Someone would have the option to sleep only when another awoke.

The following days would be filled with unloading supplies and loading up machinery and other inventory that needed to be repaired for the next rotation. Unlike other research stations like the American's McMurdo in Antarctica where there was zero left behind, the Saturnian Space Agency only returned people, recyclables and equipment to Earth. Solid waste and other undesirable leftovers of human habitation that would normally be shipped off of Antarctica at the end of the season got inventoried for research purposes, and then jettisoned out into space.

On the third day, Zander took yet another tour of the station, checking-in with everyone as she went through every space, module, and compartment on every deck. Aside from being head scientist and crew leader, she was also responsible for every bolt and every volt. Zander was an exceptional leader; up to the challenge of responding to every demand of this one-of-a-kind space station.

Consistent with the systems seen on a water-tight human habitation such as a submarine, this space station had an oxygen generator, air scrubbers, electrical power, battery backups, full computer system backups, communications, propulsion, a fully-stocked sick bay, galley, sleeping quarters, a communal head, laundry facilities, a gym, potable water, gray water recycler, solid waste disposal, environmental controls for heaters and ventilation, fire suppression, refrigeration, a space for worship, redundancies and, in some cases, triple or quadruple redundancies.

But what made this station unique was the myriad of additions, improvements, alterations, and further experiments that revolutionized space travel as we knew it. This space station had solar power, a solid-state gravity generator, electro-magnetic propulsion, a small machine shop with raw materials and an ample inventory of spare parts for the station, a hydroculture setup that included aquaponics for raising eighty-five orange tilapia fish (a livebearer that can be easily sexed and separated for population control) in a three-hundred gallon tank with symbiotic plants like lettuce, basil, rosemary, thyme, cucumbers, tomatoes, peppers, red onions, snow peas, strawberries, and watercress growing in sieved crates on top of the water; high-pressure aeroponics for tubers like red potatoes, greens, carrots, and even kiwi berries (*Actinidia argute*), and an ornery blackberry bramble; and passive-method hydroponics throughout the station with plants like edible flowers, bamboo, mint (the pineapple mint was a big hit, but the lemon mint, chocolate mint and spearmint were also favored) and Italian flat-leaf parsley where any passerby could just pluck a leaf and pop it into their mouth. And, unlike any other space station in the history of humankind, this one had an apiary of Carniolan honey bees. These docile creatures provided honey, the only sweetener on station, and pollination for every flower that needed it. And they, as well as their larvae, were edible.

Humans speak more than 5,000 languages; more even than there are species of mammal. English was the *de facto* language that was used in every procedure manual, communication, and legal document but, in conversations amongst the crew on the space station, many of whom were multilingual, it became common to hear and learn phrases from the native tongue. In the common areas you'd hear, through the years, Greek, Korean, Vietnamese, Croatian, Danish, Polish, Gaelic, Romanian, Finnish, Pashto, Russian, Yiddish, Swahili, Afrikaans, Spanish, Navajo, Italian, Farsi, Mandarin, Cantonese, Arabic, German, Portuguese, and Thai… "Pass the book." "Would you like some tea?" "Where's the dog?" and "Fuck if I know," were commonly learned phrases. Then there were sign-languages, Morse code, Braille, maritime flags and pennants… People were rarely monolinguistic, and these scientists and explorers were hungry for the stimulation of knowledge. At one point in our history, more than thirty university sports coaches were paid far more money than anyone else at those institutions, including the professors. But now, once again, education, scientific facts, and exploration won over unchecked agnotological befuddlement: We were succeeding one again.

Other successful experiments had been implemented like algae lamps, night and day LED lighting to assist with maintaining circadian rhythms as well as multicolor LEDs throughout the station for visual stimulus or to celebrate birthdays and holidays; textured bulkheads that offer a passerby tactile stimulus; a spectacular audio/visual system with extensive catalogs of online games, college courses and lectures, movies and television programs as well as music and meditation for auditory stimulus and cognition that could be controlled in each compartment; and, for the sake of the lonely human heart, there was a mixed-breed mutt of a dog named Punk on board, but she got too old and was taken off-station a year back and, to the crew's dismay, had not yet been replaced. Puck was a young mutt in the process of being trained (along with the normal puppy training, Puck's tolerance was being tested for a vegetarian diet, just as Punk's had been) before being transferred to the station on the next rotation, but that was not to be.

A few times a week, on her first walk-through of the day, Zander would pluck five or six mint leaves as she passed by, and then hide them in different compartments on the station. After lunch, on yet another walk-through, she'd take Punk with her to find them. "Find it, Punk!" then, in an excitable "Let's get ready to ruuuuumble!" voice, *Find iiiiiiiiiiit!*"

Punk was a champ, and sorely missed. Sometimes, though, when Zander watched her lick up a wilting mint leaf then return to her for her next command, she'd think of how much of a shame it was that humans took the fierce, wild wolf and controlled and contorted it into any shape, size, color or purpose they felt best suited them, the human. In Punk's case, they turned the vicious "alpha dog" carnivore wolf that used to roam the terrain in packs, howling at the moon, into a small, tame, obedient, mixed breed herbivore whose only challenge in life was to find miniscule mint leafs on a space station.

"Ah, humans," Zander thought, as she closed another hatch, "someday, we might prove to not be as smart as we thought we were all along. Hope I'm there to see it." Then she laughed at the sheer stupidity of that idea. "Check that. I want to be miles away when we figure that one out."

CHAPTER 2

ZANDER

Zander was content on her walk-through until she opened the door to the head. Marcus and Echo were sitting on the deck, and in front of them lay a disassembled toilet. "Ah, crap. What the hell happened?"

"Nice choice of words," replied Marcus.

Echo shrugged, "It's clogged, or something."

"'Or something?' How many PhDs does it take to fix the plumbing?"

"Two so far," they said in unison. "Are you offering to help?"

"I'll pitch in just a second before none of them work," Zander winked. Seriously, she asked, "That's not going to happen, is it? It's just this toilet?"

Marcus reassured, "It's just this one."

"Ok. Good deal. When you're done here, head off to medical," she said, walking away, "Aaand roll your eyes…NOW!"

Part of the company's (ridiculous) monitoring was a med-check for everyone when the new crew first arrives, three days in, and the last day aboard for the out-going crew. After that, it's every two weeks for those on-station, and monthly for those on the ground. "Research," said the company. "Overkill," cried the pincushions. In a comical act of rebellion, the ground-crew once turned in their urinalysis specimens all at the same time, all in the same cup.

Travis, whose tertiary degree was in electrical engineering, also peeked in, "Yes or no?" After getting vigorous nods from both of them, he moved on… Sixteen assents later, the space station's sound system blasted AC/DC at a concert-level quality and volume. For the next two hours, the crew went about their chores, tasks, and assignments rocking out with no complaining neighbors or sensitive doggie ears to stop them. If the Agency wanted their attention, they'd have to flash the station's lights; otherwise the *Oasis* was her own little world.

~ ~ ~

During the night, the fated "clogged, or something" toilet that was "fixed" exploded. Aerosolized fecal matter and, let's just call it gray water, splattered far and wide. Those working in the labs were the first to arrive, and those asleep in the berthing compartment woke suddenly and followed the stench.

"What the hell happened, DOCTORS?!" screamed Zander. "You said the toilet was fixed! Everyone else out! Close the door; oh God, the smell!"

Marcus, who favored collecting data in well-organized, clean-room laboratories over the chaos and filth of field work, pinched his nose closed and blinked rapidly, "There is shit everywhere! Ah! Look at what you just walked through."

Echo tried not to vomit, "This has got to be a biohazard: *E.coli* or something."

"Yet another brilliant response from a doctor," shrilled Zander.

"I'm an engineer!"

"Who can't fix a toilet?!"

"Ok: Training time-out!" Marcus made the repeated "T" sign with his hands, "We've got a hell of a mess to clean up here."

After spending hours disinfecting not only the head, but the passageways, bulkheads and anywhere else the rest of the crew pointed ("That's not poop, that's paint!"), the genius doctor and brilliant engineer showered-out, ate alone, and hit the rack, completely exhausted.

But it was too little, too late. Zander cooked their first meal, infecting some of her crew. Sex and other close-quarters activities spread the bacteria to others, and the exploding toilet finished them off: Within days, everyone became infected with the typhoid bacillus.

Days later, the relieved crew of eight returned to Earth. They were tired, as expected, but something else was wrong. The final blood tests on-station showed an increased count in white blood cells, but that could happen when the Earth crew mingled with the previously isolated station crew. Everything was easily explainable. Nothing was alarming. But *something* was wrong.

Echo, who had just returned home, was the first to show signs of illness; a headache, thought to be a sign of a low-oxygen situation. She died quickly and her crew was quarantined.

Misdiagnosed headaches rapidly became the least of the crew's problems as symptoms burned through them with fever, chills, vomiting, abdominal agony, unrecoverable shock, and unavoidable death.

CHAPTER 3

GROUND CREW

Dr. Uluru Kata-tjuta's had a diminutive body but a powerhouse brain. He was originally from Australia, but he had since become a man of the world. During his extensive travels he collected kitsch that meant something to him, but was just clutter to others.

Most recently, after a conference on communicable diseases at the World Health Organization in Geneva, Dr. Kata-Tjuta road-tripped through Vienna, Budapest, then backtracked a bit before going north through Bratislava, up to Prague, west to Frankfurt, then luxuriated with a first class ticket home. The country's capitals weren't the destination, just the pivot point to head off to another direction, another horizon.

He traveled light, with his own money, and always with a big suitcase. By the end of every business trip it was filled with wines, cheeses, cured meats, jams, honey, soaps, roadside crafts, local textiles and handmade jewelry. He traveled alone, slept alone and always returned to his loving family with suitcases bursting with gifts.

For himself, he kept items ranging from gift-shop quality rosary beads from the Vatican, to a drum from the Caribbean, a Latin American tribal mask, a prayer mat from the Middle East, a common Paralejurus trilobite fossil from the Atlas mountains of Monaco that sat next to a set of brown and white dice he's had since a childhood game of backgammon with his older brother (a tournament he will never let his brother live down), a fountain pen from England, and most recently, a cuckoo clock from Austria. The clock hung on the wall behind the good doctor, in between a bulletin board with a world map on it and a child's drawing that resembled an atom. Or was it the solar system? Who knew for sure?

The Director burst in, slammed the door closed, and demanded, "Start talking, Doctor! What is happening? Why are they so sick?"

"They have all tested positive for typhoid fever."

Ferociously impatient, "And?!"

"That was the good news, Director."

Silence.

The Director leaned over the doctor's desk and whispered with menace, "Are you going to tell me the rest, or…"

"Ok, so, listen. The *Salmonella typhi* bacterium has been in and out of our history for thousands of years. Even with a maximum fatality rate of only twenty percent, it's managed to kill people like Alexander the Great, Queen Victoria's husband, President Lincoln's third son, Olympic gold medalist John Taylor, Dr. Hakaru Hashimoto, one of the Wright brothers, and, somehow, ninety percent of Napoleon's army."

Dr. Kata-Tjuta exhaled sharply and continued, "Previously, typhoid fever was completely preventable with simple handwashing, eating well-cooked foods, boiling any questionable water, and isolation for the infected."

The doctor, worked-up by the irate Director's not-so-subtle growl, pushed away from his desk and started pacing the room, "It only recently became a superbug threat to billions of people when we forced its evolution with the use and abuse of antibiotics. The bacterium has adapted to survive our only way to kill it."

It just wasn't sinking in, and the Director was starting to go nuclear.

The doctor continued, "There's more: Among its new strengths on the station is the addition of the NDM-1 gene, a hearty, resistant, community-based gene that jumps from bacterium to bacterium in something as simple as a puddle, making previously treatable infections suddenly *untreatable*."

Kata-Tjuta looked into the Director's eyes and spoke slowly and clearly, "Our typhoid is now completely drug-resistant and alarmingly fatal."

"What? Why us? We're a space agency, not some Third World, polluted, over-populated trash heap. It's only a crew of eight, and they work in the sterile vacuum of space," the Director raged.

"Their workspaces are not sterile," the doctor rolled his eyes at the slur. "The station is anything but sterile, and they live and work in very close quarters."

"Doctor!" the Director bellowed.

"Director, it's even worse than it appears. I looked it up. Atlanta's Centers for Disease Control and Prevention foreshadowed this danger in a 2013 report, and I'm quoting from memory here, 'Drug-resistance in *Salmonella typhi* has jumped significantly - from about twenty percent in 1999 to more than seventy percent in 2011. Because antibiotic resistance occurs as part of a natural process in which bacteria evolve, it can be slowed but not stopped. These threats will worsen and may become urgent. If that ability is lost, the ability to safely offer people many life-saving modern medical advantages will be lost with it.' Although," the doctor exhaled, "it appears that it is no longer a question of 'if'."

The Director, who was a pusher, a problem solver, and a force to be reckoned with, suddenly realized the magnitude of the situation.

Blinking rapidly at Dr. Kata-Tjuta, as if to erase the images presenting themselves, the Director sank into the nearest chair: The two crews would die. And with them, most likely, the Saturnian Space Agency was doomed as well.

On the wall behind the doctor's desk, the cuckoo clock struck twelve noon. Or was it twelve midnight? Who knew for sure?

Returning to Medical Quarantine, the doctor checked-in with the team. Everyone was devastated by the quickly declining health of the ground crew.

Marcus was the guinea pig on Earth when the specialists tried to find a cure for those sick and dying on the space station. He and his grounded shipmates were given the best medical care possible, but suffered unshakeable high fevers and died surrounded by people, but alone in their sweated delirium.

Fear and panic spread as quickly as the fever.

CHAPTER 4

TERRENE RUINATION

The term "Typhoid Mary" refers to the infamous Mary Mallon who eventually died of pneumonia in a forced quarantine in 1938. She was the first person in the United States to be described as someone who was a *carrier* of a disease but not sick by it. Mallon was a cook for seven families in New York, moving on when entire families became ill with typhoid fever soon after she started working for them. When this trend was noticed, she was investigated. And, after she obstinately refused to give samples for medical testing or stay in quarantine, she changed her name and moved on to cook for others (contaminating their food during preparation because she didn't believe in washing her hands, even after being warned that that's how the illness was spreading), killing more than fifty people before she was finally forced to live out the rest of her life in quarantine, dying there at age sixty-nine.

Zander remained stone-faced while the Director was on-screen, but as soon as she clicked-off, she shuddered by the news that she was, in fact, a Typhoid Mary. In less than three minutes, she escaped to the furthest compartment on the station. And, once there, she shut the hatch and dogged it down, making sure it was sealed tight before she screamed at the top of her lungs.

She caught her breath, and screamed again. Her grief was wretched and profound. She stayed until her fists were skinned to the bone and her blood ran freely down the bulkhead. She stayed until her toes were broken. She stayed until her vocal cords ruptured. She stayed until her strong and healthy body was consumed by the black void of grief.

Uselessness overwhelmed her and irreparable nothingness violated every cell in her body. Zander, our highly-regarded, over-achieving, respected-by-all, truly fearless leader, destroyed herself until her physical body was the only thing left of her. She died on the station by a suicide pill from the guilt of infecting her crew who, all but one, had died in screaming agony right in front of her.

Dr. Feis, the sole survivor on the station, was infected, but showed no symptoms: Feis was a carrier. The space network cast the doctor away in efforts to reverse-quarantine Planet Earth. When given the choice of hypersleep or suicide pill, Feis chose hypersleep.

Just as the Director had predicted, the Saturnian Space Agency was gutted. It failed.

Once the leader of the pack, it was now tainted with a plague, it's crew died in their care, and their space station was adrift on an ocean much the same as a derelict life raft, afloat with a dying sailor after the ship went down. The sharks, sensing blood and death in the water, were circling.

Feis's family rallied hard for the doctor's return, giving the once-robust Saturnian Space Agency a bad name.

Eager to separate themselves from the debacle, they sold the *Oasis* to Archduke Hork Aetna, a greedy billionaire, whose most notable hobby (known to the general public, anyway) was to buy his way through the red tape for the rights to host modern games in ancient fields and arenas. He didn't want modern arenas like Madison Square Garden; he wanted ancient landmarks that hurt others to submit to his ego, his money. He really was one of the most ridiculous people to ever attain political power and he notoriously preened for the attention of the public, usually at the expense of those very people. On the flipside, if you gave him a million dollars to ignore dangerous ecological studies, then he'd add you to his close circle by making you a top advisor, probably even in ecology or agriculture: His loyalty was that shallow.

Many more suitable arenas were standing empty after bullfighting was outlawed, but they were just too easy. He wanted to humiliate history. Rome's Colosseum once again opened its gates to rabid fans who witnessed, for the first time ever, a tennis tournament right where gladiators had been once ripped to pieces by lions. And, at the Grand Ballcourt of Chichen Itza, where a whisper could be heard more than ninety meters away, screams of, "GOAL!" were shouted after a football player scored. Badminton was played in the most ancient theater in the world, the Theater of Dionysus, which lies practically in the shadow of the Acropolis. And, said to be the steepest ancient theatre in the world, Pergamon in Turkey was opened for, of all things, arm wrestling tournaments. Money was to be made, and if it enraged or humiliated the public to do so, then all-the-better it was for ultracrepidarian Hork, his family, and their cronies.

He told Dr. Feis' family that he would save Feis, when the reality was he couldn't care less: All he wanted was the station. He pressured the Agency into selling it to him, and when they did, quarantine was broken when Hork's crew took over the station and brought Feis's sleeping capsule back to Earth.

The *Oasis*, was then staffed with unfamiliar people, disinfected, restocked and restored.

The plan was to break Earth's embrace and head out into space. That was the goal all along, with the Saturnian Space Agency's program, but the *Oasis* wasn't ready for independence.

Humanity's knowledge was insufficient; their diets were too restricted and dependent on plants that died, the water tanks and reclamation system were too small to maintain the volume needed to sustain anything other than the station's occasional sixteen inhabitants, plus thousands of other problems that were never addressed because it was just too soon.

Aside from that, Hork and his kin had over-populated the small station with more people than she was ever tested to hold.

The death blow: There was no other port in the storm, just Earth. *Oasis* was never intended for interstellar travel, just interplanetary, with Earth as her home-base.

The once mighty space station, viable, picturesque, and promising, had surpassed the point of safe return and, like an oasis in the desert, the space station eventually dried up, mercilessly killing its unfortunate inhabitants.

Even if they had returned, the vapid Earth wasn't doing much better. Dr. Feis, rescued from slumber, became the new Typhoid Mary, infecting the population that had no resistance or treatment for this bacterium.

That caused a domino effect. Funds for space travel with other agencies started to dwindle to unsustainable levels.

Life on *terra firma* went from bad to worse: War, poverty, pollution – your basic apocalyptic recipe for humans destroying whatever is within their grasp.

The dream of living off-world in space or on another planet – hell, another *moon* would have sufficed – died of typhoid fever.

～ ～ ～

"So, we are dying? Is that what you're saying?"

"If you mean humanity then, yes, we are dying. But it's much worse than that."

"The sky is falling?" the Interviewer smirked at the camera.

"Chicken Little mistook a falling acorn, so that is not a suitable analogy," the Environmentalist said. "If you want to characterize this situation, might I suggest using Cassandra?"

"Isn't she the one who pissed-off Apollo?"

"Very good," the Environmentalist nodded. "Hell hath no fury like a displeased god. Apollo fell for the maiden Cassandra's beauty and, in efforts to woo her, gave her the gift of prophecy, but when she rejected him, he cursed her. From then on, she could foresee disaster but her prophecies were never to be believed. In my field, it's been referred to as 'Cassandra's dilemma.'

"Environmentalists have been screaming from the rooftops for a century about pollutants, toxins, dangerous gasses, noise, over-population, deforestation, strip-mining, heavy metals, chemical spills, coal ash, plant and animal extinctions…"

"Blah, blah, blah!"

The Environmentalist stopped talking, turned to the camera and deadpanned, "Cassandra has arrived."

The Interviewer snorted with derision, but one of the camera operators barely managed to stifle a chuckle.

"Are we done here, or may I speak?" Environmentalist asked politely.

The Interviewer got up to leave, but the Producer disagreed, so the filming continued.

With disgust, the Interviewer sat back down with a huff, plastered on a fake smile, then gestured with a wave of a hand that the Environmentalist may continue.

"Now," the Environmentalist said, "A major mass extinction occurs when more than seventy-five percent of plants and animals die out within a specific span of time. Each of the previous five major mass extinctions, as first identified by scientists Sepkoski and Raup, usually occurred over millions of years and were caused by natural global occurrences, like the well-known Chicxulub asteroid impact sixty-six million years ago that triggered the Cretaceous–Paleogene extinction. On a world-wide level, it took out everything from terrestrial herbivores and carnivores to plants that relied on photosynthesis and animals that relied on phytoplankton. That event is also known as the Fifth Extinction.

"The current span of time, which began after the last what you would call 'Ice Age' about twelve thousand years ago, is referred to as the Holocene epoch. It has witnessed a massive loss of plant and animal species mostly due to humanity's impact. We didn't kill off the mastodon in the beginning of this time period, but deforestation, overfishing, fisheries bycatch, poaching, low genetic diversity in endangered animals…"

The Interviewer yawned.

"…Human overpopulation, plastics, antibiotics, water pollution, air pollution, light pollution, toxic waste, strip mining, global warming and so much more, have caused what scientists see as anywhere between one-hundred to ten-thousand times greater rate of extinction than seen in any of the previous five major mass extinctions.

"The first mammalian species to go extinct due to human-induced global climate change happened in 2016. It was the Bramble Cay melomys, an Australian rodent that succumbed to rising seawater overtaking its short, tiny island on what used to be called the Great Barrier Reef. It couldn't possibly be coincidental that in that very same year, twenty-nine percent of the Great Barrier Reef died, and ninety-three snowballing after that. Hundreds of plant, insect, and animal species became extinct every day. No one noticed, and no one cared!

"In 2017, the third-largest iceberg ever recorded calved off of the Larson ice shelf in Antarctica. Evidence was all around us, but when the U.S.'s Environmental Protection Advocacy removes all of their climate change information from their website, then launches programs to *unscientifically* challenge the very idea of climate change, well… It's as stupid as when former U.S. president Theodore Roosevelt took his son to Africa, in 1909, on a 'conservation mission.' By the time these two men had completed their 'mission' they had shot and killed five-hundred-and-twelve wild animals, many of whom later became extinct. Roosevelt was so proud of himself, and his son, that he included a tally of the dead in a book he published the following year. It's blatantly obvious that we don't *protect* plant and animal species, we *endanger* them!

"Then, in 2018…"

The Interviewer's attention wandered off like a moth after the flame had been blown out.

"…By 2020, even the dolts could see the truth. The early estimates were that we'd lose species at the rate of one for every six in existence. As far as we can tell, they were correct. One-in-six plants and animals! Our fault; *we did that!*

"A single mammalian or reptilian species' population can go from healthy to extinct in an expected window of five-hundred to ten-thousand years," the Environmentalist dug in deep. "But, humanity cut that timeline down to a mere century. And it's not just a single, stand-alone endangered animal that perished – it's thousands of documented flora and fauna, and those, again, are just the ones we could observe. The cute baby snow leopard…"

The Interviewer perked up a bit.

"…and the leatherback sea turtle's eggs hatching on a tropical beach are the awe-factors of extinction, but they are only the tip of the iceberg…"

The Environmentalist watched as the Interviewer's eyes rolled and head lolled back in utter boredom. It was an all-too-familiar scene. A camera operator's jaw popped during a long, frustrated yawn. Even the Producer was about to call it a day.

"…As hundreds-of-thousands of less tangible or cuddly plant and animal species died out just as quickly, or humanity weakened them so severely that the next time a natural disaster, like a drought, occurred, the entire species would be so depleted that it could not survive and recover from what was once just a speed bump in its evolution.

"We really didn't need kill wild animals to satisfy palates, quotas, egos, superstition, religion, or fashion-trends. It was a sickening list; otter, beaver, harp seal, fox and big cat pelts; rhinoceros horn; elephant ivory; colorful bird plumage; bison tongue; shark fins; gorilla hands; whale oil; wild tropical fish and live coral for our stupid fish tanks; infant animals torn from their families for decades of grim servitude in our circuses, aquariums, and zoos; exotic animals for our homes with no mind to their nee…"

The Environmentalist saw the Producer hand-signal the Interviewer to regain control of the conversation, but before the vacant Interviewer had a chance to process and react appropriately, the Environmentalist quickly finished, "Diversity was our planet's biggest treasure and we've ruined it! We humans are witnesses to the Sixth Extinction: The Holocene Extinction."

It took a full fifteen seconds of dead silence, and the Producer's dry cough, for the Interviewer to realize that the Environmentalist had stopped talking.

Straightening up, the Interviewer blinked a few times, focused again on the Environmentalist, and asked, "Is that all?"

It took a full five seconds for the shocked Environmentalist to comprehend what the idiot had just asked. "'Is that all'? Are you serious?"

"Yes," the Idiot nodded.

"Do you have any questions for me about the biological annihilation?"

"No," the Idiot said.

"I, uh," the flustered Environmentalist stuttered, "I guess we're done here, then. It's over."

~ ~ ~

Not five years later, typhoid fever decimated humankind, and not long after that it completely eradicated them. Even if there were carriers that didn't get sick, the survivors were too few and far between to pull humanity out of its death spiral. Once again, Dr. Feis became the sole survivor as the world's population completely succumbed to this extinction-level event.

For lack of better harbinger imagery, Nyx had arrived to usher human beings into the darkness of their downfall. The faint, soft, helpless cries of millions of fevered people were witnessed by no one but themselves.

All countries went dark but for a mere handful of lights that represented a single human being in fifteen or so isolated locations around the world. They wrote in their journals, talked to the dead, or looked to the stars, each believing that they were the last person alive on Earth. Then, one by one, those last lights flickered out.

The superbug *Salmonella typhi* destroyed humans, and humanity's greed, indifference, and stupidity consumed the Earth to her near death with an environmental collapse after the tipping point was reached from global warming, loss of habitat, resilient pests, overpopulation and the like, bringing about the Holocene Extinction; the end of humanity's timeline.

~ ~ ~

A day, a century, or a thousand years later, aliens arrive. They populate Earth and sooth her wounds. These aliens become the new dominate species, the new Earthlings for a new epoch.

END

PART II

A POSTERIORI

CHAPTER **5**

THE EPITOME OF THEIR DOWNFALL

At the same time, on another Earth in another Universe, the same crises occurred, decisions were made, but things didn't end so well…

The Saturnian Space Agency performed what had become routine; eight people were on their way to relieve the entire crew of a low-Earth orbit space research station. Unbeknownst to all, a pan-resistant superinfection *Salmonella typhi* had arrived with a healthy-looking crewmember. For one week, both crews mingled, everyone became infected and then the crew that had been relieved flew home.

Misdiagnosed headaches rapidly became the least of the crew's problems as symptoms burned through them with fever, abdominal agony, unrecoverable shock and unavoidable death.

As the sole survivor on the station, the one known as Feis was infected, but showed no symptoms; the doctor was a carrier. The space network abandoned Dr. Feis and the space station in efforts to quarantine their problem. When given the choice of hypersleep or suicide pill, Feis chose hypersleep.

The Saturnian Space Agency was gutted. It failed. Once the leader of the pack, it was now tainted with a plague, all but one of its crew died in their care, and their space station, *Oasis*, was adrift.

23

The lifeforms that needed humans to tend to them on the *Oasis* eventually died from neglect.

The fish overpopulated, cannibalized, suffered disease, and then suffocated in clouded, putrid water.

But before the fish had their last gasp, their symbiotic plants, growing in crates on top of their water, withered mawkishly and died, turning into stink and slime.

The bees, naturally comfortable with swarming, needed a kind soul to keep their hive in check. Because they were unable to fly off to find food elsewhere, they overpopulated quickly and perished when the greenhouse's health declined.

Throughout the station, the hydroponic mint, parsley and edible flowers simply wilted and dried-out on the spot after they drank every drop of moisture left in their water trays that had previously insisted on daily attention.

The blackberry bramble, once known as Kristy, exploded in size. Its barbed wire tendrils ascended the walls and abseiled to the floor, anchoring, curling and poking its way into its neighbor's light and water source.

The tubers multiplied quickly, weighing down its support apparatus until it buckled; everything else survived until the sprayers could offer nothing but air.

Eventually, because there was no one left to complete the task of recycling and replenishing the water tanks, the levels droughted-out as the plants drank their fill, and then evaporated until the tanks were bone dry.

To end it all, after the diagnosis of *Salmonella typhi* was confirmed, the ship's dehumidifier was set on high, in hopes that the dry air would prove to be inhospitable to the bacteria. The flourishing, verdant *Oasis* was transformed into an arid desert as barren and infertile as the surface of the Moon.

The world's only surviving space traveler orbited a diseased and dying Earth in a solar-powered, hard-wired vessel, asleep and unaware that, far below, all that Feis had ever known was burning its own funeral pyre.

CHAPTER 6

COLD DESCENDS

In this other world, more than thirty generations had passed. Many of humanity's hopes and dreams had never panned out: Einstein's unified field theory, space elevators, reality simulators, and cryogenics, to name a few.

Those were just things that they couldn't *add* to this world. There were many others that they managed to create, but then couldn't erase no matter how frantically they backpedaled.

Humanity's numbers had swollen to unsustainable numbers, even after repeated pandemics, blights, famine, holy-, civil- and world wars, and then they collapsed, within a few generations, to numbers resembling the early 17th Century.

This population was different than any of its ancestors in many important ways, giving it a chance not to just survive, but to thrive and succeed as three-hundred billion other people in its history had failed to do. That's how many lessons it took for these humans to learn this: *Three-hundred billion.*

Geographically speaking, hard-won and devastatingly lost geopolitical boundaries of the world were now nonexistent, in this long reach of time; there were no more countries to speak of. Instead, there were mutually understood danger zones, dead zones, and quarantine zones; all uninhabitable due to pollution. Many other countries ceased to exist simply because they never survived the rising ocean water.

Life was so fragile that it was an honor to be among others, not a rite or rule. Many people, or even entire clans, were nomadic, often visiting established settlements; others were established and welcomed the nomads. Food, clothing, and tools were shared with strangers to extend each other's social networks.

The nomads wandered the globe in search of clean water, fertile land, and clear skies. This was usually accomplished by moving further up the mountains, closer to the source of rivers. Others moved out into the deserts. More than a few bands headed to the true north and south poles. The magnetic poles had long since shifted away from what had been once considered North and South in the 20th Century, and with the warming temperatures, the ice caps had melted away leaving Antarctic free of ice, and the Arctic a large saltwater sea.

Early on, humans returned to the animals. Racehorses and luxury lapdogs were a thing of the past; descendants of Clydesdales and smart hunting dogs like Labradors and terriers prevailed, although true breeds had long since vanished.

They used heavy horses to plow the fields, tow the wagons, fell the trees, and fertilize the crops. The Amish style of living was mimicked and put to good use. Even after that culture had faded into history, its influence could be seen in the harnesses, saddlery, bridles, horseshoes, buggies, wagons, plows, and barn-building in this new age.

Metals other than iron were forged, too. Copper was their antimicrobial, killing on contact even the most pathogenic of the superbugs created and feared centuries before, and aluminum could be recycled and reused infinitely without any degradation to its matrix.

Much like the Comanche Indians in the American West, this neo-humanity had no central government, just loose gatherings of people all living and working together. *Ad hoc* committees of elders were created to decide on community issues. The elders (both female and male) met to discuss issues, but orders were never given, just advised. There was no shouting or anger, hatred or violence.

This other world studied its history to help plan its future; specifically, the 20th and 21st Centuries were scrutinized because that's where so much had gone wrong. As with most laws on Earth, it had been more about rights, and less about responsibilities. The late 19th Century felt like the beginning of a boom, but it would have been better described as the beginning of the Age of Decline and Death.

These critical centuries were the commencement of destruction and waste on a planetary level. They were marked with rampant quomodocunquize that, in turn, helped usher in the demise of the largest animal to have *ever* existed: The blue whale. The last one seen was mortally wounded when a cargo ship collided with her out in the open ocean. Godspeed, Mother Nature.

At the turn of the 21st Millennium, humanity was, almost intentionally, de-evolving. Worlds of information and education were available to so many people who could have *done something positive* with it but chose, instead, to once again believe that the world was flat. This madness was self-inflicted.

For some, nothing would change their minds on even the most essential circumstance; for others, all they needed were facts and scientific evidence. Then there were the double-dealers; many politicians, lobbyists, industries, and corporations were well aware of the truth, but chose to follow the power, follow the money.

While investigating the blue whale's doom, this other world's neo-humanity learned that the horrors they were currently combating so many generations later, had all started in this earlier "prosperous" era.

This world never grew potatoes on Mars or mined any moon, and the Great Barrier Reef became known as the Dead Reef Barrier. They knew they were stuck here, on their own planet, in their own filth, because of decisions made centuries ago. They had to make the best of what was left to them.

What this new population didn't know was that their efforts to raise themselves from the mire were probably going to be brief, but ultimately, futile. It was like looking up to see the peak of Everest from Camp IV; so close, so beautiful, so clean. But they've had to walk past piles of shit and the dead, frozen bodies of Rainbow Alley to get there. Neo-humanity had reached the Death Zone. Even if they make it to the top of the world, their stay will be brief, and then gasping and spent, they must survive the trek down, back to the dead bodies, back to the shit, and back to life as they had known it.

What had decided their fate was the fact that, as enlightened as humanity was with the internet at their fingertips, human rights as their war cry, and science on their side, 'because we can' was their driving force, their motto, their license, and their *carte blanche.*

There had never been more slavery or human trafficking than there was in the 21st Century. And, for the first time ever, there were just as many overweight people in the world as there were underweight.

By this time in our history, the Earth was so polluted that there was even more plastic in our oceans *than fish.*

World-wide unemployment was one the rise and more people were living in slum cities with lack of access to electricity, education, medicine, clean water, and proper sanitation. This wasn't just limited to co-called "Third Worlds" anymore; it was becoming mainstream. The list of doom was as tragic as it was long, and empathy for others was plummeting. Murder was on the rise; as was suicide.

The last useful drop of oil was extracted from the Earth in 2049. This inevitable and foreseeable oil crisis fed unimaginable wars and political strife.

Countries weren't just *addicted* to oil, they were physically, and socially dependent on it. If their supply was cut by just fifty percent, then they could expect a nationwide stoppage like New Orleans after Hurricane Katrina in 2005, but no one would come and save them, no matter how many days passed. Education? Commerce? Emergency Services? Football? All gone. Crime? Are you kidding?

For America and other nations, *oil was freedom*, and it was worth protecting by military force, if necessary. As it became scarcer, pipelines callously trumped indigenous people's legal rights, and endangered natural habitats and water-ways not only with their construction, but also with their devastating spills that had already been coldly worked into the budget plan and insurance years ago as mere "breakage."

Hydraulic fracturing of subterranean fissures in a last-ditch effort to extract oil and natural gas from the Earth had caused sinkholes and earthquakes where there had never been any before. The buildings and infrastructure of municipalities that were not up to seismic codes were suddenly suffering dozens of quakes where there weren't even opposable tectonic plates. It was the water that was lubricating the ground; these tremors also occurred when dams were built. More water meant more area earthquakes. These were *manmade* disasters. Progress is not ever guaranteed.

The "can do" attitude continued on, and soon after Americans started giving birth to microcephalic babies due to the Zika virus that used infected *Aedes* mosquitos as a vector, government-sponsored, wholesale insecticide spraying began without much consideration to any other "bug" out there.

The mosquitoes survived the decades of efforts to eradicate them, but the first unintentional heavy casualty in this war was the honeybee. Almost immediately, they began to die out in record numbers. As a result, more than half of the food and drink offered in most grocery stores simply vanished from the inventory, including chocolate, dairy products, many fruits, and to the horror of billions, coffee.

The second heavy casualty was the water. Mosquitoes use standing water in their life-cycle, so this was a target for the sprayers. The insecticide was, for all intense and purposes, main-lined into the water table resulting in many-a silent spring.

In this other world, contaminated water wasn't new. At one point in its human history, up to forty-five million people died every year just because they didn't have access to clean water.

These new humans, these survivors of the Age of Decline and Death had many problems to overcome; many wrongs to right.

Finally, ingenuity was celebrated; hostility was tempered; this Earth, with her flora and fauna, was protected and all people were cherished.

Even the food was different. What was once considered a "chemical shit-storm" of artificial, processed sustenance was, once again, basic nutrition which provided a solid, sustainable foundation for growth for all.

Around the world, museums had been broken into and the education gleaned from them became the new Information Highway.

It wasn't artwork that attempted to save humanity; it was the Inuit and the Bedouin. It was the Amish and the Aboriginals, it was the Indians and the Celts, it was history and culture, science and nature.

New-humanity's decisions were so different from their predecessors; they had to be different in order for them to survive…

CHAPTER 7

THE HUMAN CONDITION(ING)

It was discovered that in this other world's distant history, hatred and prejudice were naturally so boring that groups used to have to liven things up to excite (and incite) its members with Crusades and Inquisitions, holy wars, watching "witches" burn at the stake, public stonings, tortures, assassinations, beheadings and hangings, honor killings, cultural fatwas, Nazi and Neo-Nazi rallies and songs, the Klu Klux Klan's lynching and cross burning, the Islamic State's destruction of idols, the Taliban and al-Qaida martyrdoms, or the trusty go-to tactics of blacklistings, boycotts, censoring, and censures.

Religious and cultural prejudice was so unnatural to them, that the haters required not only blandishments, rhetoric, and propaganda, but also signs pointing to whom they were supposed to hate.

It was so unnatural that people not only had to be told whom to hate, but also why. They needed to see the Star of David pinned to a Jew's clothing, or the Scarlet "A" on a shamed woman's dress.

One was deemed to be superior to those with breasts, or this nationality, or that disability. To fit into one's society, or to avoid the same condemnation, one was required to loathe the dark skin, or abhor those with a "native" appearance, or wrong accent. We didn't like *them*, and then they became *us*, and then *we* didn't like *them*.

Oh, the names that they proudly created and used to freely and publically show our disgust… *Coolie! Nigger! Spade! Darkie! Paki! Pikey! Spic! Redskin! Injun! Wetback! Goy! Kike! Dago! Kaffir! Gook! Native! Rag Head! Camel Jockey! Kraut! Wop! Taffy! Polack! Wog! Faggot! Retard! Bitch! Whore! Slut! Cunt! Heathen! Blasphemer! Infidel! Heretic! Freak! Primitive! Savage! Half-breed! Half-wit! Untouchable! Slave! Street rat! Beggar! Refugee! Immigrant!*

They were fools, all of them: The haters were fools for their rampant, obtuse dystopia, and the lovers were fools for ever thinking that they would live to see the haters change. The haters were the reason it took so long. The snark, the snear, the slurs, the smear; stupid, foolish people.

Mongoloid, Negroid, Caucasoid, or mixed: It doesn't matter!

It doesn't matter whether or not one chooses to pray, to whom one chooses to pray, or where one chooses to pray. Atheistic, agnostic, monotheistic, polytheistic, Christian, Muslim, Hinduist, Buddhist, Sikh, Jewish, Bahaist, Confucianist, Jainist, Shintoist, ethnic or indigenous religion, any other religion past or future, paganism, omnism, or even secularism: It doesn't matter!

Female, male, cisgender, intersex, or transgender: It doesn't matter!

Heterosexual, homosexual, bisexual, asexual, or pansexual: It doesn't matter!

Clothing, accent, food, custom, language, skin tone, hair or eye color, body weight or height, asymmetrical face or body, place of birth, education level, birthmarks or congenital disabilities, birth order, body defects due to illness or accident, fertility level or choice, sickness or cleanliness: It doesn't matter!

Socioeconomic level: It doesn't matter!

IT. DOESN'T. MATTER. *Homo sum humani a me nihil alienum puto.*

Humans matter. How they treat each other matters. How they treat animals matters. How they treat their environment matters. How they treat something or someone who has no say in how they themselves are being treated matters. And, lastly, how humans behave when they think no one will find out matters.

Violence became the way of life. Not the violence of a predator on the savanna taking down a zebra, but choreographed hand-to-hand fight scenes, gun battles, tanks, ships, jets, bombs and minefields, kidnappings, sexual abuse, physical abuse, verbal abuse, animal abuse, anger, aggression, force, rioting and warfare, all became *normal* and *expected* in movies, television, the internet, games, music, books, and even t-shirts and bumper stickers. This fantasy-level of heighted terror was considered *entertainment!*

It became so ingrained in their daily routine that it soon became real life. Dangers and destruction happened so often that they became indifferent and fatigued with every passing horrific event, yet it continued to escalate. It became so heightened that it only had one more place to go: It became passé.

In this other world, humanity began to shy away from adrenaline-fueled, hate-chasing, catastrophic violence. It no longer wanted to experience blood-spilling, senseless, egocentric rage against fellow human beings. Or, animals, for that matter.

As if by an overnight agreement, bombs stopped dropping on cities, guns were cleaned and stored away. The world's military forces went home and paramilitary police forces simply walked the streets to check on neighbors, lending a hand where they could.

It was not a forced shutdown.

It was not a cease-fire agreement.

It was an all-out, world population meeting the apex of cataclysmic vehemence and realizing the next step.

Peace.

CHAPTER 8

FISCALLY FERACIOUS

In this other world, they had learned from the mistakes of others; and they had a lot to learn because past mistakes were, at times, incalculable.

After the Agricultural Revolution and a few Industrial Revolutions, being human became an easier thing to do. They lived longer (twenty years longer just by having access to toilets!), and more luxuriously than ever before, and more of their offspring survived birth, infancy and childhood than any previous generation.

In fact, the speed of which humans multiplied made the idealized breeding cycle of Fibonacci's rabbits look like that of the periodical cicada. Before long, many more humans were being born than were dying; creating an unsustainable overpopulation surplus of 140,000 people per day, or about 51 million people every year. That's more than the entire population of the state of California, with 40 million, or the country of South Korea, with 50 million, at the beginning of the 21st Century.

As a result of the Agricultural and Industrial Revolutions, money and goods started rolling in; as did the waste. Like never before, people were discarding old and buying new without a thought as to where it was coming from or even where it went. Decades later, it was cheaper to buy new than fix what was broken, and not long after that, it didn't have to be broken to be thrown out; it was discarded because a better version had come along. And, the next year, something even better. The effects on the natural world were devastating.

Crippling the rush to save Nature from wonton destruction was the shifting baseline syndrome. People of one generation would accept the world they were born into; that was their baseline. Then next generation would accept their own ideas of nature and natural, even though what their generation inherited was much worse than the last. And, the generation that followed them accepted *those* changes in Nature as their baseline. One generation would say, "We've always been cutting down the Amazon; nothing's changed." Another would say, "We've been shark-finning for years; nothing's changed." Each would believe that because it's "always" been done, then there's nothing wrong with it; it's natural, it's sustainable. Generations have "always" known smog, over-fishing, and penicillin. They won't grasp the situation's cause-and-effect until it's too late.

Falling under the category of "too little, too late," was the human interest that finally peaked about recouping their resource losses to landfills.

Dangerous landfills were loaded with a trillion dollars' worth of recyclables, a billion dollars' worth of perfectly recyclable electronics, and hundreds-of-millions of dollars' worth of items that could be resold or repurposed, as well as millions-of-tons of compost. Plus, if something that'd been landfilled could be reused then that would prevent the carbon footprint of a new item being manufactured and sold on the market.

A few decades into the new millennium, private companies began to form with the purpose of mining the landfills. The landfill miners did their best. They'd dress in hazardous material suits and start at one end of a landfill, moving through to the other end, sorting out metals, papers, plastics, electronics, *et cetera*, to recycle, and household, gardening, industrial discards like bricks, shovels, wooden pallets, *et cetera*, to resell, upcycle, or repurpose. So much landfilled waste was as good as the day it was discarded because it hadn't been exposed to air, moisture, or the sun's ultraviolet light.

In the Digital Age, paper (most of which would never be referred to again) contained ninety-five percent of the world's information. And, at one point in history, twenty-seven thousand trees were killed every year just for toilet paper! It's not just the trees that were saved for every ton of paper those landfill miners pulled for recycling, it was also seven thousand gallons of water and over six-hundred-and-fifty gallons of oil.

Other discards, such as smartphones, contained seventy-five elements from the periodic table. If it could be harvested from the landfills, then manufacturers didn't have to go back to the mountains to mine the elements in their virgin state. There was so much buried in landfills that a computer company once recovered about 2200 pounds of gold from smartphones. That haul alone was worth more than $35,000,000 USD. In fact, one ton of smartphones would yield 300 times more gold than one ton of gold ore!

Mining the landfills brought about jobs to every participating economy, even to the previously shunned populations like the inner cities. Automation had a profound effect on the human workforce, leaving millions of people jobless, but computers knew that string could pull, but only humans knew that string couldn't push. Computers could read a barcode, make breakfast, draw up legal papers, and rule the assembly line, but only a human could sort through the trash and see the value of aluminum, chromium, copper, gold, iron, lead, lithium, mercury, nickel, platinum, silver, steel, tantalum, tin, titanium, tungsten, and zinc, as well as glass, wood, paper, cardboard, plastics, Styrofoam, furniture, electronics, appliances, organics, clothing and brick buried in landfills. The idea of mining our landfills for their recyclables could have worked, if only they had started sooner…

This other world's consumer-created landfills weren't the only greedy result of humanity's burning desire for more. After an unimaginable number of domestic chickens were devoured by humans, chickens went extinct. Preceding them, turkeys, too, went the way of the dodo.

Unrestrainable outbreaks of avian flu across Asia, Africa, Europe, and the Americas, finished off what humans were going to have to stop consuming anyway. The drive for bigger, juicier, meatier, cheaper, and more, forced the hearty chicken through a sieve of genetic alterations, antibiotics and hormones that produced oozing tumors and ghastly deformations in the fowl. These unsightly birds were still processed and eaten for decades by consumers who were blissfully unaware that "white meat" doesn't necessarily mean "breast meat."

Unclean water, horrific egg-laying facilities, grinding useless live male chicks into chicken feed, and the money-driven need to get from egg to slaughterhouse within weeks rather than months pushed this false bird to its inevitable and bitter end.

Of the wild birds that survived the virus, global warming, habitat loss with urban encroachment, deforestation and flooding, and not being hunted to extinction for their meat, eggs and feathers, two species became regulars at the dinner table in this new era.

The first was the pigeon. As it turns out, they appeared to be harder to kill-off than the cockroach. These weren't the tender, hand-raised squab, but the city-dwelling, statue-shitting birds of old.

The second bird species that proved to be resistant to humanity's devastation was the seagull; the "rats with wings," as the sailors used to call them. They knew how to survive; move inland, away from the plastic oceans. And now, neo-humanity was serving them up as "seabird *au vin*," or just herb butter for the simpler palate.

Many things were simpler now.

CHAPTER 9

DERECHO

Themyscira put her hands behind her head and leaned back in her chair, "I think 'Rosie the Riveter' screwed women over."

"Rosie the... What?! Why? She was *empowering* to women. Why would you think such a thing?"

"She was a social icon created during one of the first world wars... World War II, I think, to urge women into the industrial workforce after so many millions of men left it behind to join the armed services and fight overseas."

"Exactly! Because of her motto, because of that historic poster by J. Howard Miller, women stepped up, especially in the defense industries," Kintsukuroi insisted. "Women dug in. Women welded, hammered, assembled, produced, packaged, and forged hundreds of thousands of aircraft, jeeps, rifles and machine guns, not to mention ships, ammunition, tanks, and tools; the list goes on."

"It was government-produced propaganda, pure and simple," Themyscira insisted.

Kintsukuroi was quiet, trying to figure it out. Finally, she had to say, "You lost me."

"Think about it: America's involvement in two war fronts during World War II needed a tremendous amount of soldiers, sailors, Marines, and airmen, right?"

Kintsukuroi was interested now, "Right."

"When those men left, the civilian workforce was in dire need of an equal amount of people to fill all of those abandon factory jobs, especially considering that the war was going to need more manufactured goods, ships, airplanes, tanks, and conventional weapons than the country had ever needed in peacetime. Agreed?"

"Agreed."

"But now the population left behind was, for the most part, made up of children, old men, the disabled, and women. Are you still with me?"

"Yep, keep going," Kintsukuroi moved her chair closer to Themyscira's. "I'd really like to know how Rosie failed women."

"Ok, so now the U.S. government had another problem. How do they fill-in-the-blanks? Child-labor laws were in effect, so that left only the old men, the disabled and, of course, a healthy population of hundreds-of-thousands of women.

"In the early 1940s, most American women were housewives, and if they worked outside of the home, then they were artists, nurses, teachers, or secretaries. Anything outside of this narrow purview was not welcomed. Yes, women – or 'girls,' as they were called—were scientists, pilots, and medical doctors, but those few women could be counted, begrudgingly, only in scores compared to a number along the lines of one million men. These trailblazing women were not respected by superiors, peers, or anyone who might have to work under them, and they were not given the same advancement opportunities or pay as men."

"I know all of that. But where does 'Rosie the Riveter' sucker-punch American women? I don't get your point."

"She wasn't just a cultural icon, she was their hero," Themyscira said softly.

"What?"

"The government heavily recruited this new workforce by printing posters of Rosie, with her sleeves rolled up and flexing a bicep, telling women it was their patriotic duty to leave their buckets and mops at home and go work in the factories to support the war effort, very often doing so against their husband's or father's wishes.

"Except that it wasn't just factories," Themyscira continued. "There was a nation-wide vacuum-suck of jobs due to the loss of the male workforce. Women were suddenly working as something more than just someone else's assistant. They worked entirely new jobs and succeeded (*and even excelled!*) in fields in which they had no prior access, interest, or training, and their efforts on the homefront allowed men on the warfronts to win the war and come home to them."

Kintsukuroi became impatient, "True, true and true. But…?"

"What happened to the 'girls' after the men came home?"

"I don't know."

"What happened to the men after they came home?"

"I don't understand what you want me to say," Kintsukuroi slouched in her chair, "And you are giving me a splitting headache."

"When the men came home, they wanted their jobs back. And, they wanted their women back in the kitchen."

Kintsukuroi was just about to give up on this conversation, but she, instead, gathered herself together and asked, "What does this have to do with Riveting Rosie?"

"The government used her to empower women, telling them it was their duty to enter the workforce to support their men, their country, in this trying time. 'You can do it!' she said, and women did. They did it for years! And they did it well.

"Right about here, in the timeline of the evolution of Western women," Themyscira continued, "women were coming into their own. It was a critical, a most crucial, moment in history for them, and had they been allowed to continue, it's possible that they would have earned the respect of the opposite sex. They would have been seen as valued colleagues and women rather than viewed as a threat to a man's friable ego or frangible masculinity and intentionally demoted and referred to as 'girls' to remind them of their place and dependence on the male sex."

Themyscira's took a deep breath, then exhaled sharply, "But once the war ended, the government had another problem. The men didn't like competing with women in the workforce. The men didn't like late dinners or dirty laundry. And the men most certainly did not like 'girls' earning almost as much money as they did.

"So, once again," she continued, "The government rolled out the propaganda machinery and *hundreds-of-thousands* of women were fired, (*fired!*), even though more than half of them wanted to remain in their jobs, after the war was over.

"Imagine firing a half a million women just because men wanted their jobs! They told these magnificent women that they were now expected to return to their former lives as housewives or lower-paying librarian jobs. It was their duty to leave the work force and return to their homes, return to wearing skirts, return to mopping floors, and doing dishes. It was their duty to marry their war heroes, buy tract homes and have babies. Do you know what happened next?"

"Obviously not."

"These women excelled so incredibly, once again, that the generation they produced was referred to as Baby-Boomers!"

Kintsukuroi was quite for only a moment. "So, you're saying that 'Rosie the Riveter' empowered women and sent them working in jobs that had never before even been an option to them. They did well. In fact, they did it so well, that once the war was over, these new, strong, bread-winning, empowered, economically emancipated women had to be shamed out of their jobs and told it was now their duty to return to the lower-paying workforce jobs they originally held as a seamstresses, dancing girls or magician's assistants (or no job at all) before heeding Rosie's call. Women, or 'girls' as they were called to keep them down, were manipulated twice-over, and Rosie lead the charge. Is that what you meant when you said that you believed 'Rosie the Riveter' screwed women over?"

"That is what I meant," Themyscira said, exhaling a huge puff of air. Her shoulders sagged with grief in memory of those long-lost women.

"I agree," Kintsukuroi whispered. But then she nudged her friend and said, "Do you know what happened *after* they gave birth to the next generation?"

"Obviously not."

"More women went to college and earned a degree than ever before in the history of humanity."

Themyscira gasped, "Is that true?"

"Yes, it is. In fact, for a long period of time, more women were enrolled in college than were men, and more women than men *graduated*. Even as doors still slammed in their faces, and even as their pay was less than their male counterparts, women educated themselves and succeeded in the corporate world, in the financial world, in the political world, in the technology world, in the scientific world, in the media world, in the entertainment world, in the world of academics, in the world of medicine, and in the worlds of law, order, and national defense. Not all of these women came from traditional two-parent homes, and not all of these women raised their own families while married. They weren't the ones telling themselves they shouldn't do it."

"Or couldn't do it," Themyscira added.

"Right! These women, and not just American women, by the way, bucked the system that was screwing them over. They fought those that held them down, kept them back, and called them 'girls' to make them feel inferior.

"Once empowered with their own destiny," Kintsukuroi continued, "they became astronauts, and generals, marine biologists, and commercial pilots, captains of industry, and board leaders, patented inventors, and published authors."

"Professors. Sheriffs. Judges. Senators. Heads-of-state," Themyscira smiled.

"Yes. Yes. Yes. Yes. And, yes. These women now had choices. They could have families, they could have careers, or they could support their families with their careers. They could continue their education, or work in their desired field with the degree they had. They could work in those very same factories and shipyards as architects, engineers, supervisors, managers, or department heads. They could be entrepreneurs, founders, and owners. They could buy their houses, save money for retirement, financially support their children, their parents in their later years, or even a spouse if need be. In other words, these women were self-sufficient. No one need tell them whom to marry. No one required them to have children. No one told them where or how to live their lives. They could, if they chose, do as they're told, or they could, if they wished, become autonomous."

"That explains why they were held down for so long: It's easier to control someone who has no choice in life but to do what they're told." Themyscira was sad once again.

"But no more," Kintsukuroi said, "we are whole now, and better than ever."

"Yes, we are." Themyscira, a passionate woman with immense empathy for those in trouble, looked over at her friend.

Kintsukuroi had turned back to her work, but her posture had changed; she was shining with renewed strength and vigor. The conversation had been good for both of them; Themyscira rolled her shoulders back, lifted her chin, and smiled.

"Yes," she whispered softly, "we are."

CHAPTER 10

TRIBAL...

I n this other world, Hesiod thought about the whole of humanity for quite a while, and then turned and asked the cavernous empty classroom, "Why was it really so damn difficult to see a woman as a woman, and not as a girl, property, a fuck, a slut, or a whore?"

Hesiod was sullen and silent, trying to organize these tumultuous thoughts and emotions.

"And, if they have the audacity (and the power) to say no to a man's advances, she is then known as frigid, an ice queen, or a lesbian, even if none are true.

"Long before Muhammad (peace be upon him) walked the Earth, and even centuries ahead of the emergence of the Judeo-Christian faiths, men began their legal fight against women. This was then dovetailed into mainstream religious doctrine and continued on for thousands of years in perpetual lawmaking. What was once comfortably egalitarian was now overwhelmingly *Patriarchal*.

"The earliest known law codes, dating back to 2400 BCE, were inscribed on two clay cones known as Enmetena and Urukagina after the reigning kings. Within these codes lie the details of the first documented laws against women. One of them even promoted violence against women stating that, 'If a woman speaks out of turn, then her teeth will be smashed by a brick.'

"Later, in the days of Mesopotamia, the Code of Hammurabi (again, named after the ruler), dated 1754 BCE, gave the first indication of

Patriarchy. Fathers and husbands now *owned* their daughter's and wives' sexual reproduction. Virginity was now a condition for marriage, and rape was focused more on the loss of viability for marriage for a daughter because she was damaged goods, rather than seen as a crime or trauma for the girl. Only wives were put to death for adultery. Male honor was sacrosanct and protected by law seemingly above all else.

"In the 12th Century BCE, the Assyrian's inscribed one-hundred-and-twelve laws; more than half of them related to marriage and sex. Wholesale female oppression, for the first time in recorded history" Hesiod murmured, "became the legal right of the husband. He could pull out his wife's hair, pawn her, or throw her out on the street, and the wife of a rapist could, herself, be raped as penance for the sins of her husband. And if this were true, why would he care? He could just go on raping, and if caught, his wife would pay his fine. This was the birth of the *legalized* rape culture. Girls meant nothing; women, even less so. I imagine that those violated women felt tremendous guilt and terrible shame when they learned that reporting the rape caused the rape of another woman; she also knew that her rapist felt no remorse or shame and would, himself, never suffer a punishment or public shame.

"The law numbered forty (of these one-hundred-and-twelve laws) was the kicker. It was a mark of *social classification* 2,000 years before it became a mark of religious faith. It clarified a woman's station in society at a glance, and set down laws that could be legally enforced with savagery if a woman stepped out of line. It was judging a woman by the clothes she wore, rather than by who she was in her own right. This is something," Hesiod remarked with disgust, "that went on for scores of centuries.

"Law Forty," the teacher continued, "written in the 12th Century BCE stated, 'Married women, widows and Assyrian women must not go out on the street with their heads uncovered. Daughters of the upper classes must be veiled with a veil, an abaya body cloak, or a long robe. The concubine who goes out on the street with her mistress must veil herself. A prostitute must not veil herself. Her head must be unveiled.' Women were sorted and graded according to their stations in life, and each of the five classes was identified by what they wore. This was later purified into binary thinking: A covered woman is pure, and an uncovered woman is evil (and needs to be beaten into submission by the nearest man). This, in turn, lead to further thinking that became twisted into religious doctrine: A woman was either pure (rare in religious texts, and extremely – if not impossible – to attain), or she was seen as bad, evil, the fallen, *the reason for the fall*, or a whore (these are all much more common representations of women throughout history, but particularly observable in religion).

"In a Patriarchal society, a woman's contribution to society was rarely recorded unless it was with a negative connotation. Or, childbirth.

"And, it was the ancient Athenians who created many of the veils that were still in use far into the 21st Century; the *himation* covered the woman's hair, the *pharos* covered their hair and lower face, and the *tegidion* was a full-face veil with only eye holes to show the human underneath. It was the fear of a woman's body that powered these veiling laws through so many religions, societies, and customs, millennia after millennia. Could you imagine a man subjugated to such laws? To me, that sounds as ludicrous as subjugating a woman to them, but back then…" Hesiod's voice quieted down.

"Celebrated philosophers of ancient Greece, like Aristotle, saw these cloaked, silent, submissive apparitions as sub-male or imperfect men because women "leaked" with menses, and were open during intercourse and child-bearing and semen didn't flow from them as it did men, and these scholars believed that semen was the essence of a man. This was seen not as *differences*, but as *weaknesses*.

"One noted philosopher even saw women as a different species!

"Aristotle himself said, 'It is the mark of an educated mind to be able to entertain a thought without accepting it.' If only he had seen the error of his contemporary's treatment of women rather than going along with it; merely entertained that thought, rather than accepting it as truth…" Hesiod mumbled.

"On a side note," Hesiod spoke up, "throughout history, many conquering nations saw the people they had just conquered as sub-human or as a different species – it made them more heroic and their victims easier to subjugate.

"These great thinkers all supported the idea that women were incapable of reason, and therefore must be chastised and controlled, just as if they were children. They believed that only men had sophrosyne, meaning a soundness of mind and superb character which, in turn, meant that they also knew their limits, were pure, and had self-control. In their minds, women inherently lacked these qualities.

"As another form of control, the honor of the household was held within the women, so any transgression, such as a female speaking too loudly in public, meant that it was up to the man of the house to remove shame and restore honor. Remember the teeth-smashing brick?" Hesiod asked the empty room, "Same thing here.

"There was even a law on the books in Rome that allowed a husband to divorce, or even *kill his wife,* for the crime of... drinking wine. Yes, you heard me correctly; *drinking wine.*

"These laws, these customs, these beliefs justified oppression over women and waves legal, iron-fisted, domestic violence, including child abuse. From these seeds of socially-acceptable Patriarchal behavior, medieval Judaism, Christianity and, later, Islam grew."

Hesiod sat quietly for a moment before continuing.

"Routinely, when skeletons were unearthed by archeologists, like the Siberian Ukok Ice Maiden dating back to 400 BCE, they were deemed to be male if they were found to be buried with weapons and arrowheads, but when sex could eventually be determined by skeletal markers, and later DNA, it turned out that this particular ice warrior was *female.*

"The archeologists were shocked by this revelation, but science had done its best: If you are buried with the items of a gatherer, then you are a female, and if you are buried with items of a hunter, then you are a male.

"This rigid 'obligatory function of male/female pairing' train-of-thought continued on to other parts of the animal kingdom; scientists were later stunned to find out that male seahorses give birth, and that a lifeform as complex as a female komodo dragon can produce offspring asexually with parthenogenesis (virgin birth), even in the presence of fertile males.

"It was the age-old dogma of the sexes, and it was reinforced in every echelon of every mainstream society for thousands upon thousands of years: Politics, law-making and enforcement, religion and superstition, military, medicine, academics, agriculture and farming, manufacturing and commerce, entertainment and fashion, tradition and social mores were all endorsed, supported, and perpetuated sexism. The next generation was watching.

"Even when we became more enlightened, achieved goals of higher education, and were free to be who we wanted to be, boys still had to play with blue trucks, and girls still had to play with pink dolls; nothing was purple. Except, of course, that in the Ice Maiden of Ukok's nomadic society, where life was more precarious, roles weren't set based on biology."

"On a side note: Although there were not as many restrictions on men as there were on women, the male social construct could be just as needlessly fierce."

Hesiod turned to open the windows, feeling for the cool breeze of the morning.

"When the Holy Roman Empire spread far-and-wide, female-led societies were particularly at risk to brutality because Roman law did not recognize the authority of a woman as a leader, much less as a warrior.

"This underestimation, Emperor Nero discovered, was a terrible mistake, and he learned this lesson well when he invaded Britannia. Among other losses, including thousands of troops, Queen Boudicca of the Celtic Iceni tribe *burned the 20-year-old city Londinium to the ground* in the year 60 CE. Two thousand years later, the Boudicca destruction layer still survived thirteen feet below what was then called London.

"Yes, Nero eventually won, and yes, the Holy Roman Empire went on to rule Britannia for four centuries, but he, Emperor Nero Claudius Caesar Augustus Germanicus, of the Holy Roman Empire, had to defeat a woman first."

Hesiod sat down heavily and murmured to the empty room, "We will finish this lecture tomorrow. Class dismissed."

CHAPTER 11

...WARFARE

"Did you know that men dream of men even more than women dream of men? And that's universal – across all walks of life, all socioeconomic levels. All ages. All cultures. Don't you think that that's odd?" Hesiod asked, as the clock rang the hour.

"Males dream of other males more often than females dream of males. I think that that's truly bizarre. I doubt it's all rainbows and hero-worship, though. I bet that quite a bit of it is fear-induced and maybe even some hatred.

"Never mind. On with the show...

"While ancient Egypt considered *companionship* the purpose of marriage," Hesiod continued from yesterday, "rather than reproduction, and Egyptian queens could rule in their own right, China and other Asian countries saw to it that men were meant to be the authority and allowed outside, and that women were to be obedient, quiet, and never permitted to leave the house.

"Before Vietnam was invaded by China, who then ruled for nine hundred years, by the way, men and women were equal. A woman could even have two husbands. After the invasion, the Vietnamese became second-class citizens, and women were somewhere under that.

"During China's Han Dynasty's four centuries, Confucianism promoted a deep social hierarchy and it was fiercely Patriarchy. The Confucian Classics (China's equivalent to the Torah, Bible, or Quran) governed all rules of conduct both inside and outside the home.

"The *Liji* was the Confucian Classics' book of rights. The absolute power of this text speaks of the proper way of wives and mothers, explaining their three obedience's to their father, their husband, and to their grown sons, and that their proper place was inside the home, 'nei'. Men, it explained, belonged to the outside, 'wei', with its commerce, business, culture, government, and education. 'Men should not speak of what belongs inside of the house, nor women of what belongs outside.'

"Two-and-a-half-thousand years of Chinese history and culture were documented in the *I Ching* divination carving dated at 175 CE. In it, you would find that Heaven was thrown into chaos if proper roles of men and women weren't obeyed. This balance was the key to peace and order.

"As I understand it, at one time, and for thousands of years, 'yin' was believed to be female, negative and dark, (not in the least, was this meant to be derogatory) and 'yang' was believed to be its exact opposite; male, positive and bright. They were perfect opposing forces that worked in unison as principles; equal, interdependent, and balanced in harmony with each other. Complementary. Do you understand?" Hesiod asked the class. There was no answer.

"This held true until the Han scholar Dong Zhongshu made yin inferior to yang in the 2nd Century BCE. This meant that human females were now considered inferior to males, and that it was now, suddenly after all this time, *divinely* ordained to be so.

"This is not an original thought. It's quite a timeless, and apparently indefatigable, story of men giving themselves the benefit of god on their side when they set the rules of conduct in peacetime, as well as times of war, but also when one rules, or explores. Even when one experiments, occupies, or enslaves.

"Anyway. These oppressive ideas inspired laws that were spread throughout Chinese-conquered lands and continued until the in-rush of Buddhism by way of the Silk Road.

"Buddhism (and Taoism) brought, I believe, a breath of fresh air with its female deities and salvation for all, regardless of gender or race. It was well established in China by the time of the Tang Dynasty in the 7th Century.

"Fighting it, every step of the way, was a wave of Neo-Confucianism's cultural and social theory, and political philosophy. Among its horrors, was something known as Chinese foot-binding." Hesiod shuddered involuntarily.

"Chinese foot-binding was done to *every* little girl from the Palace to the fields, and consisted of, without exaggeration, snapping a fully conscious child's foot in half and folding it under so that her toes pointed towards her heal, then binding the foot tight in an effort to stunt the natural growth as the girl matures. After the snapping, twisting, and binding of one foot, the other foot was done the same way.

"Then, possibly as often as every day (*for years!*), their feet were unbound, fractured again, if need be, cleaned of debris (up to and including lost toes that have rotted off), and then bound back up, even tighter than before.

"The idea was that the smaller her feet were, the better she'd marry. A woman's tiny, child-sized feet in dainty silk lotus shoes were deemed erotic to the man; her painful mincing steps as she walked around on the heels of her feet caused her hips to sway seductively. Also, and more realistically, it crippled her for life, and that kept her at home or in the fields, and out of politics and commerce. That is, of course, if she survived this horrific, repeated assault to her body.

"Empress Consort Wu Zetian, who died in 705 CE, defied the prescribed order of the atypical Yin/Yang, promoting both men and women equally within her government, including making a former palace slave, Shangguan Wan'er, the first female Prime Minster in Chinese history. This office would not be held by a woman again for the next *1,400 years*. Years! Patriarchy; a shining example," Hesiod's head shook in utter disbelief, as if just hearing this for the first time. "Fourteen centuries. More than *fifty generations!* Unreal.

"After the Empress' death, her niece, daughter, and prime minster were all murdered, and the Tang Dynasty, after this brief interruption, resumed its rule.

"Interestingly, when the Tang Dynasty finally collapsed in the 10th Century, women were blamed for it because they had apparently displeased Heaven. Incidentally, I believe that this was often the reasoning for *any* failed dynasty in Chinese history.

"For reasons and logic beyond me, Empress Consort Wu Zetian was the only female to rule as Empress in her own right, in more than 4,000 years of Chinese history. It would be another thousand years before another female would rule China, although as regent rather than in her own right, with Empress Dowager Cixi in the late 1800s. Both women were praised, and both were torn down, smeared, and slandered. Not because of their personalities, character, decisions, piety or beliefs, but simply because they were women.

"It was Cixi, after 1,000 years and an estimated *one-billion* girls affected, who finally outlawed foot-binding. Perfidious Patriarchy," Hesiod finished with a hiss.

"When China invaded Japan, Confucianism clashed horrifically with Shinto. Shinto, which was ruled by a female deity (the sun) whose brother was the moon, was the exact opposite of the Yin/Yang paradigm.

"But by the 11th Century, Japan was becoming self-ruled, and the Chinese Emperor was merely a figurehead. At this time, in this world, women lived apart from men, inside, while men conducted their life outside, conversing with each other but separated by *kicho* screens. I can't answer the obvious question, because I just don't know...

"These cloistered women were educated and artistic. Among many other accomplishments, the craft of the bonsai tree was born; they brought the outside world inside, beautifully miniaturized.

"Another shining moment: Murasaki Shikibu, born around 978 CE. Her real name is unknown; Murasaki, meaning violent, is a character in one of her stories, and Shikibu reflected her father's status. She wrote, 'The Tale of Genji'; to be forever known as *the world's first novel*.

"But then, the Age of the Samurai began in 1185, and lasted until the late 19th Century. Its laws overruled the aristocratic government and Japan was again ruled by men's fondness for a sharply Patriarchal society. Women lost what little they had until well into the 20th Century."

Hesiod walked back and forth a few times, and then stopped at the wall of windows, looking out.

"Elsewhere, the Middle Ages saw the end of Antiquity, and the rise of Judaism, Christianity and Islam, but no less were the rigors on the definition of the female. Women were seen as unequal, less, weak, and unworthy. New religions, environments, philosophies and laws all saw to it that the role of women was diminished and powerless. And, it had to be so because it was ordained by God.

"Interestingly, all of these different gods had the same disdain towards women. In essence, Man and the rest of the Universe was brilliantly Created (including female animals), but Woman dramatically fell short by any measure.

"Why would an All Powerful create something so sub-human, fragile, emotional, delusional, depressed, hysterical, unbalanced, illogical, weak, agitated, difficult, deceiving, seducing, obstinate, socially unacceptable, immature, stupid, loud, shameful, inherently evil, and disgusting, to be the mate of One's pride and joy?

"'I have made Man, and Man is awesome. Now, I will create the mother of his children. She will mean nothing to him, for all he will need of her is her hole. I'll make her meek and brazen, whorish and virginal; she will be, she MUST be, his downfall!'

"St. Jerome said, 'Woman is the root of all evil.' But, fortunately, his opinion didn't matter and his words never carried much weight." Hesiod looked at the rows of empty seats.

"That was sarcasm. He was a Biblical scholar and preparer of the Vulgate version of the Bible used by the Roman Catholic Church. In this book, it was made clear that marriage was the only refuge from evil for women.

"The truth is, St. Jerome looked down on marriage as well, and once said that 'Marriage is good for those who are afraid to sleep alone at night.' It was the chaste virginal female, or nothing. Except that, even then, he said, 'Virginity can be lost by a thought.'

"This moment in time echoed like so many before it. Anything other than being a wife and mother was seen as too ambitious; if she wanted more, then something must have been wrong with her. If something excited her, then she was hysterical. This was never said of men.

"The new religions had assured us all that women had two classifications, the pure virgin, and more likely the evil, fallen, and the root of all evil. Politicians, religious leaders, judges and juries, all male, of course, had complete say over what a woman could do with her body, whether she could divorce her husband, or whether she could even speak. It was forced invisibility. Again.

"'A woman should learn in quietness and full submission. I do not permit a woman to teach or to assume authority over a man. She must be quiet.' The Bible's Timothy 2 11-15. This meant that a woman could never become a preacher or have any power within the Church. This intolerance is ancient and time-honored.

"In the 12th Century, Hildegard von Bingen fought for things within the Church that were still being fought for into the 21st Century. She wrote of her visions in a text called 'Scivias,' and nine centuries later, women still represented only twenty percent of the world's power, even less so in the worlds of religion.

"'All of you are, were, or will be whores, whether by intention or action,' is a line from 'Roman de la rose.' It was *the most popular* poem of the Medieval era. It's no wonder that, at that time, 'singlewoman' was slang for prostitute.

"Christine de Pizan was educated when education for daughters was irrelevant. She, the first consciously feminist person, countered 'Romance of the Rose' as it's called in English, with 'The City of Ladies.'

"It defends women, proves all of the good things women have done, and explains what women could do, if educated. She believed that one could judge a society by how it educates its women. She was correct, as it turns out; the societies that educated their girls who, in turn, were productive in the work force as adults, had *sizable increases* in their productivity and gross national product which, in turn, stabilized their respective countries far-and-above what an all-male society could do.

"Many queens, like Elizabeth I of England, read this book. 'Your Royal Highness,' and 'Your Majesty' are both gender-neutral, so she became gender-specific: The Virgin Queen. And she used language to maintain power by saying, 'I may have the body of a weak and feeble woman, but I have the heart and stomach of a king, and a king of England, too.'

"If she married she would have given up power as queen, to the inherently more powerful king, but instead of becoming outranked by a husband, she claimed her autonomy by remaining the Virgin Queen, ruling England and Ireland for nearly four-and-a-half decades. British queens after her ruled even longer with Queen Victoria's reign lasting for sixty-three years, and Queen Elizabeth II surpassed her own Sapphire Jubilee's sixty-five years on the throne.

"Succeeding Queen Elizabeth I, in 1603, was King James I who famously authorized and financed the *most printed book in history*, the

King James Version of the Bible. Although he had nothing to do with its writing, he did author other books that fondly displayed his Patriarchal ideology. And King James, himself, presided over witch trials.

"'Demonology,' published by King James in 1597, proclaimed that women were more likely to succumb to demons because their bodies leaked and were weaker than men's.

"All told, the witch trials of the mid-15th to the 18th Centuries numbered in the hundreds-of-thousands, most of which ended in executions of about a half-a-million people, and eighty percent of the accused victims were women.

"Great Britain's Witchcraft Act of 1735 stayed on the books for centuries, and was used when society's upper crust tried to cleanse the riff-raff of, 'ignorance, superstition, criminality and insurrection.'

"Most of Europe's population was illiterate, and this was an age of anxiety: Fear of a woman's sexuality, fear of evil, fear of loss of power. And this was not just in the minds of Christians…

"Islam gives women certain rights, including education and property, but keeps them as second-class citizens.

"Medieval scholar Al-Ghazali called women a 'blight on the earth,' and goes on to say, 'Their deception is awesome and their wickedness is contagious; bad character and feeble mind are their predominant traits…'

"A woman's sexuality was a destabilizing threat and veiling, punishment, and seclusion were practiced as a result of these baseless, slanderous fears."

Hesiod spun around and shouted with revitalized energy, voice echoing in the empty room, "Did men do such a good job when societies were Patriarchal? *Machismo massacred!*

"For thousands of years, it was said that it was *God's claim* that men had rightful providence over females, animals, and the Earth, but (not surprisingly) that benefited only men, while being *wildly and shockingly detrimental* to females, animals, and the Earth!

"Men accepted the stewardship from God, but not the responsibility or respect due to their supposed charges. In place of this, a myopic, male-biased, tortured history commenced: More power, more money, more property, more sex, more sons. It was *parasitic Patriarchy*!

"The men proclaiming that muscles beat all never realized that the geniuses, geeks, and nerds of the world had made billions of more dollars than any top athlete had ever made in the history of the world.

"And a man, sitting motionless in a wheelchair," Hesiod shouted, "briefly explained the Universe in a nutshell, and a woman became the first writer in *history* to earn a billion dollars as an author!

"Muscle can beat someone into submission, but a brain can set them free! All of those things that, through the ages, men told women they couldn't do were incorrect. Of course women could do them. It wasn't the *woman's* deficiencies that were at fault, it was the *man's*. When society permits women to succeed, women will – and the only thing on Earth that that terrified was weak men!

"A woman's ability was irrefutable," Hesiod paced, once again, "and undeniable no matter what the reasoning of an oppressive culture might have been.

"Women were, in truth, Olympic champions in scores of sports, including those that teamed them with men. They were equestrians, race car drivers, college professors, neurosurgeons, international lawyers, federal judges, commercial pilots, motorcyclists, coaches, award winners, editors, journalists, scuba divers, conductors, accountants, captains of industry, mission commanders, project leaders, leaders in fashion, scientists, military veterans, mathematicians, engineers, architects of castles and memorials, educators, flight directors, stunt people, daredevils, hunters, world-record holders, adventurers, firefighters, paramedics, police chiefs, musicians, chess grand champions, comedians, filmmakers, directors, producers, set designers, film editors, sound editors, animators, painters, carpenters, programmers, breadwinners, heads-of-family, heads-of-state, religious leaders, self-sufficient mothers and widows, single or never-married working professionals, and self-made millionaires and billionaires.

"Women were the first computer programmers. Dr. Grace Murray Hopper, a former admiral in the U.S. Navy lead the team that created COBOL, the first user-friendly business computer language. And, in her 20s, Hollywood actress Hedy Lamarr invented a frequency-hopping device which made World War II codes unbreakable, and it was the forerunner to the wireless Digital Age, but she didn't receive recognition for her patent until she was in her 80s.

"Women helped create the world we lived in, whether men wanted them to, or not. Margaret Knight was granted the patent for the flat-bottomed paper sack, in 1858, after a man stole the idea from her, declaring that she *couldn't possibly* be an inventor because she was a woman. Stephanie Kwolek was a chemist who invented Kevlar®. Giuliana Tesoro was an organic chemist with 125 patents to her credit. Marie Van Brittan Brown patented the first home security system. Amanda Theodosia Jones invented the Jones' Process of vacuum-sealing canned foods. Flossie Wong-Staal was on the team that discovered HIV and her work lead to the creation of the world's first HIV test. Egypt's Azza Abdel Hamid Faiad invented a way to transform plastic waste into biofuel. India's Seema Prakash discovered a way to cheaply clone plants. Shirley Jackson's work contributed to communication inventions like the revolutionary use of fiber optics. Rachel Zimmerman invented a way to help people with communication difficulties. Patricia Bath revolutionized a cataract treatment by patenting a laser. Bessie Blount Griffin, a World War II physical therapist, invented a way to help disabled veterans feed themselves. Deepika Kurup was a teenager when she invented a water purification system powered by the sun! Maria the Jewess, as she was called, the first true alchemist in Western society, created the prototypes for pressure-cookers and instrument-sterilizing autoclaves. Josephine Cochrane invented the dishwasher. Mexico's María del Socorro Flores González discovered a way to diagnose a suffering patient's invasive amoebas. Sarah E. Goode, born into slavery, was the first black woman to receive a patent from the U.S. Patent and Trademark Office in 1885. *Women did that!*"

Hesiod paced the room, almost said something, but kept silent and continued to pace. After a few more laps in front of the classroom, "Why weren't there more women in government?" Hesiod asked the echoing hall.

"What were their opinions on birth control, reproductive rights, marriage rights, health care, equal opportunity and equal pay, the environment, animal rights, education, military and veteran spending, infrastructure, national parks, caring for the elderly, the disabled, and the poor, jobs and the economy, foreign policy and world affairs, ocean exploration and space travel? *WHERE WERE ALL OF THE WOMEN?!*"

Hesiod paced in front of the many rows of seats, back and forth, troubled, "Some cultures said that a woman couldn't leave the house without a male escort, and certainly they were not permitted to leave the house without head-covering and failing to comply with one or both of these restrictions could easily lead to her injury or death either from outside forces or – *stunningly* – her own family.

"And, while billions of girls and women were forced to submit their obedience to their fathers, husbands, and sons, other women were blasted into space with their fellow astronauts who were men to which they were not married, not of their culture, not of their religion, and to which those three criteria weren't even considered to be mission-critical."

Hesiod typed three words commonly used to describe females in these societies, and then scratched them out: ~~Wife, mother, daughter.~~

"She was *someone*. Her connections to a man don't determine her value. Her worth is intrinsic and innate *in her*, not her uterus, not her body. Women are not baby-making machinery. Women are more than a just a host or a vessel for childbearing. Women are more than cooks, housecleaners and childcare specialists. Women are something other than a wife, a mother, or a daughter. Women could do that, but also so much more! There is more to a little girl's destiny than maturing into a brood mare.

"Physically, women may not be able to lift as much, run as fast, or jump as far as men, but their bodies can withstand blood-loss dangers better than men's bodies due to their body's routine recovery from their monthly menses as well as being genetically gifted to survive pregnancy and child birth trauma, sometimes more than ten times in their lifespan, with one remarkable woman having twenty-seven pregnancies and giving birth to sixty-nine children, with only two not surviving childhood. And, a woman's naturally higher body-fat content enables them to withstand prolonged sun exposure, cold weather dangers, adrift on water emergencies, and starvation situations longer than a man."

Hesiod paused for only a second, "Children inherit their intelligence from their mothers. And, girls mature much faster than boys in general, but one important task is the neural pruning that takes place during puberty. Every healthy brain eventually makes the choice to discard neural pathways that the brain deems no longer relevant. This action reorganizes the brain into an efficient, capable and essential structure and brings important tasks into a much sharper focus. Girls appear to go through this process around the age of ten whereas boys appear to be delayed for as much as five or even ten more years.

"Women also live longer than men, their hearing is more acute, they have fifty percent more olfactory cells, they have more taste buds than men, and men are more likely than women to be color blind. Women are better at sensing non-verbal cues, and girls potty-train faster and learn to speak and read sooner than boys. There are many things a female does better, just as there are many things a male does better. They are *different* from each other, *not unequal!*

"Cultures, rituals, customs, social mores, and traditions are all very important to the human soul. Our tribes keep us safe." Hesiod stood in front of the vacant seats in the large classroom; the light from the far windows was still bright.

"But what do we do, what *could* we do, when our tribe no longer has the best-interests of more than half of its population? What do we do when more than half of the women murdered in the world were killed by their husbands or family?

"The opposite of a strong man is not a weak woman; it's a weak man.

"Some women can, just as some men can't."

Hesiod was exhausted. It was time to go.

"I have just shared with you everything I know about past laws against girls and women, but I urge you *not* to believe me.

"I could be wrong. I could have been misled. *I could be trying to mislead you.*

"What I have said is, to the best of my knowledge, true and correct. But I urge you to do your own research. Make up your own damn mind…"

As Hesiod opened the door to leave, but there was just one more thing to say, one more thought to share "…Your *well informed* mind."

With a soft click, the door closed.

CHAPTER **12**

NOT EVERY MAN, NOT ALL MEN

In this other world, Elena Piscopia and Cecilia Payne sat and, over their weekly tea together, discussed the lives of past women.

After a fair bit of comfortable silence, distant thoughts began to coalesce, and Elena spoke first, "A woman walking behind a man had nothing to do with her respect for him because she was *required* to walk behind him. Instead, it had everything to do with his relationship to her and *his* lack of respect for her."

Cecilia picked up on this thread, "This gender-bias was intense. Did he eat first? Was his word the last (or only) word? Did she have any say on whom to marry, where they lived, when they had sex, or if their children went to school? Was she his only wife?"

"If one thought she couldn't make those decisions because she was a woman, one would be wrong," Elena looked at her friend.

"If one thought she couldn't do it because of her culture, one would be correct. It is the weak society that holds half of its population back and threatens others if they don't do the same."

"I agree, Elena." Cecilia sipped her tea, "Many times in history, there was a king, but never a queen, and his progeny was counted by sons, but never daughters."

Elena shrugged, "If a woman chose to continue, in her life, with what was known as the 'cultural' female roll, then I'm all for it, simply because it was her own choice. *Her choice.* But flat-out forcing a girl to obey her father as a child, her husband and sons in her marriage and her sons or another male family member as a widow was just an enormous waste of human potential!"

"The obligatory gender roll of covering herself," Cecilia continued with her friend's thought, "Walking behind a man, averting her eyes, a man not looking her in the eye, acknowledging her presence, or speaking to her, disregarding education, disregarding the right to rule her own body, the right to own property, to serve her society, or to vote, was just a horrific abomination to human life."

"I agree. There was a definite slant working against females from the time they were born," Elena spoke firmly. "Even into the 21st Century, there were too many princesses and not enough astronauts. Sorry, I mean FEMALE astronauts. Not enough doctors. I'm sorry, FEMALE doctors. Too many Buffys and not enough vampire slayers. Too many pink stoves. Too many baby dolls that aren't to be played with by little boys. Too many military-based toys geared towards boys only. Too many scientific and mechanical kits not advertised for girls. Too many sequins on grade school girls' clothes. I could go on but, hopefully, I've made my point. Many ideologies worked hard to keep our faces hidden."

"Wow, well said, my friend. More tea?"

"Yes, my sweet. Thank you, kindly."

Cecilia served them both, and then returned the pot to the warmer. "Men, not God, made laws that brought the opposite sex into obedience, just as men, not God, made laws that brought slaves into obedience.

"The word 'feminism,'" Cecilia continued, "became hated because people thought feminists *hated men.* Feminism, quite simply, was the belief that women should have the same rights as men. That's all. If one believed this, then one, no matter the sex, was a feminist."

Elena, with a furrowed brow and heavy heart whispered, "Through the ages, girls and women were mutilated, hobbled, burned, raped, subjugated, bought, sold, traded, swapped, sacrificed, murdered, abused, forced, ostracized, something to score with, leered at, spied on, reduced, marginalized, killed if a girl for the sin of not being born a boy, not allowed control over her own body or reproductive rights, state-forced to abort a second pregnancy or give the baby up for adoption, or forced to have multiple pregnancies because sexual education and/or birth control options were eliminated by law, mail-ordered as brides, phone-ordered like pizzas as prostitutes, chained up or tied down, beheaded, stoned, blinded, kicked and starved to abort a baby, beaten, broken, rented, shot, stabbed, kidnapped, muted, captured and held captive, bred like cattle, cloistered, covered, fed last, hanged, starved, lashed and imprisoned for being gang-raped, legally punished for being raped, offered as an arranged marriage as young as one year old to pay a debt, settle a dispute, or perceived dishonor by way of vani, drugged, humiliated, enslaved, maimed, married-off, coerced into having sex or performing sexual acts by threatening her, her family, or others, traded for livestock, used as a form of currency to pay a debt, unite a kingdom, produce the next crown prince, and killed at husband's funeral so that he can have her in the afterlife." Elena breathed heavily to recover from the flood of emotions that had just overwhelmed her.

"*Such disrespect!*" Cecilia mourned. "Can you even *imagine* if these crimes against women still happened?! I guess Schopenhauer was correct when he said that, 'All truth passes through three stages. First, it is ridiculed. Second, it is violently opposed. Third, it is accepted as being self-evident.'"

"Unreal," Elena agreed, still recovering from her mental purge of real-life crimes against so many lost, powerless souls.

Cecilia shook her head in disbelief, "Held with equal indifference, and equal disdain, females were previously thought to be incapable, and even, alarmingly, into the 21st Century they were not given equal opportunity. They had to fight for it because they were not just fighting within their own tribes, they were fighting their own gods. Many mechanisms were implemented generation after generation to force females down. Many were *fortunate* to even be *considered* second-class citizens. It's not that women had respect and lost it; these women never even had it in the first place!"

Elena asked, "Have you heard of female genital mutilation?"

"I've heard of it, but couldn't tell you much about it. I just know that it was bad."

"Horrific, in fact." Elena took a deep breath, "Female genital mutilation entails carving out the prepuce or even the clitoris on a girl around seven years old, but could be as young as infancy or as old as puberty. Sometimes sewing the *labia majora* closed, often leaving no opening for menses or passing urine. It was performed on a half-a-billion girls well into the 21st Century in more than thirty countries in Africa, Asia, the Middle East, and most alarmingly, America and other Western countries, for religious and cultural reasons with *absolutely* no benefit to the girl and was dangerously detrimental to her health, her childbearing potential, and newborn survival rate. It was performed on dirt floors, often when a shard of glass, with no anesthesia or medical professional and no medical follow-up for infection, sepsis or other associated horrors. The procedures and their aftermaths were *intended* to be painful, because the whole point of the butchery was to keep the girl from ever enjoying sexual behavior. It would keep her chaste until marriage and because of pain during intercourse, she'd never stray during her marriage."

Cecilia pushed her tea aside. "That cannot be true. Is that true? Even if proven to be detrimental to newborns? You'd think that they'd at least respect new life. For many women, that was their sole lot in life: Baby maker. Despicable. Insane. What was the purpose of sewing her labia closed?"

"To assure virginity on her wedding night, if she survived the mutilation, that is. Her husband could slit her open with a knife before entering her sexually."

"Barbaric! Oh, those poor girls. Oh!" Cecilia became visibly upset.

Elena spoke softly, "Not every man, not all men – but, during this part of human history, there was an *overwhelming* predominance for men to dominate women. There was the male culture, destruction of community, hyper-masculinity, and false definitions. In most cases, men were the perpetrators, judges, juries, and executioners."

"I understand that," Cecilia sniffed into a tissue. "There was an *accepted exploitation* of women: Lower pay, with fewer opportunities in the workplace and higher prices for female products in the marketplace. Oddly, at that time in Western Civilization, women were the breadwinners, main consumer purchasers for the family, and primary caregivers of their single-parent families. And women often outlived men by as many as forty years; ninety-five percent of supercentenarians in the 21st Century were female. Societies should have been in awe of women."

"Instead, smart women became coat hangers," Elena said. "The press didn't know, or want to know, about women's thoughts, wishes, or ideas; they just wanted to know what women were wearing. Or, more accurately, *who* they were wearing. This all stopped. It became the designer's responsibility to record who was wearing their clothes, not the wearer's. This was mostly done through print ads and interviews, which allowed the designers and art houses to talk about their pieces better than a coat hanger or model ever could."

Cecilia continued with her friend's thought, "Women stopped allowing their bodies to be photo-shopped which had made their appearance unrealistically good, or sometimes even so bad that it looked like a caricature."

She continued, "Misogynistic advertising against a woman's perception of her own body was rampant. This ceased only when women began to exercise and eat right because they *loved* their bodies, not because they *hated* them. As a result of their actions, trillions of dollars' worth of advertising, make-up, fashion, fad diets, and cosmetic surgeries ceased to exist. It didn't go quietly. Advertisers became more aggressive, and companies that supported health and beauty became as desperate for the approval of women as women had once been of these companies. Women now had control of them, rather than the other way around."

"A woman's goodwill towards herself *and other women* was a direct threat to those making their money off of the idea that a woman hated the way she naturally looked," Elena offered.

"Yes," Cecilia nodded. "A good way to achieve this task was for advertisers to make the ideal woman unattainable. Sound familiar? 'If you are as (unimaginably) thin as we think you should be, then you are good. If you can't attain this (of course you can't), then you are bad. If you're not muscled like this, or have breasts like that, if you don't buy this, or drive that, if you live anywhere outside of this high standard, then you need our help to attain *It*, to be *It*. We will correct you, and make you socially acceptable.' Billboards and thick, glossy magazines demanded submission. Demanded obedience. Just like those laws that subjugated them. Women feared the disapproval of others above all else. They were born and enslaved by the egregious idea that they had to be people-pleasers not people-leaders."

Elena listened closely to her friend before saying, "Without falsely calling her a witch, a whore, a slut, an adulterer, a tease, a temptress, or a liar, she can choose to wear makeup or choose not to. It doesn't matter.

"Each woman has her own idea of empowerment," she continued, "her own level of modesty; it's up to her. She can choose to wear hijabs, niqabs, burqas, veils, abayas, gloves, ghoonghats, dupattas, yashmaks, scarves, saris, churidar pyjamas, kameez, kurtas, pants, shorts, skirts, dresses, swim suits, heels, blouses, t-shirts, jeans, bras, panties, or nothing at all, to express herself, her faith, her traditions, or culture. It doesn't matter."

"This led to the end of body-shaming," Elena spoke proudly. "It's not a woman's responsibility to be beautiful. Added to this, women stopped characterizing women (and themselves) as stereotypical bitches or gossips, and they started raising their children, both boys and girls, with the same ideals. Eventually, generations went by and these traits faded. Conversations weren't so catty or flippant as women became stronger, healthier, more confident, supportive, decisive, educated, and helpful to others. Young girls grew up to be women who were no longer trapped under the weight of atelophobia. This is when the women of the world became authentic, independent, and empowered; they were no longer thrilled by a man's money, they were no longer trapped by aporia, and they were now in control of their own destinies."

They sat quietly, drinking their tea, and then Cecilia inquired of her friend, "Medicine used to be based only on male physiology, the symptoms of a heart attack were based only on what a man felt, and bullying was recognized based only on what boys did. Did you know that?"

"Yes," Elena responded, "This is why it took so long for people to realize that females bully each other, often even their own friends or peers, by sniping about their appearance, gossiping, back-stabbing, rumor-spreading, or other similar undermining behaviors. These bullies were smart, they did well socially and academically, and were well-respected by adults; all of which describe the exact opposite of a typical male bully."

Cecilia agreed, "Outlook drastically changed for females of all ages when they started seeing their own worth." She sat back with her tea and continued, "and the worth of the women around them. Women began amplifying each other's contributions in the Patriarchal business world to be sure that the woman's voice would be heard and she was given credit for her ideas rather than have them attributed to the loudest man at the meeting."

"Females no longer ran each other down for not being skinny enough, tall enough, having a darker skin tone, wearing glasses, the wrong clothes or any other previously perceived fault," Elena murmured.

Cecilia picked up on her friend's idea, "They began taking turns taking care of each other's children for free when mothers had to go to class to finish a degree, and when those mothers came home, they took care of the other mother's children when those mothers needed to go to school or work or the doctor's or buy groceries.

Elena said, "This worked whether they were married or single. Single moms started living together and working together to raise their children and to better their life before they could move on. If they didn't live together, then these moms lived in close proximity, so that the children could be easily dropped off and picked up. In this 'it take a village to raise a child' effort, child-care costs plummeted, children weren't ever left alone after school and the children learned more about tolerance, acceptance, patience, and unity than the children who were left to their own devices after school or in daycare.

"This wasn't the endgame,' Elena continued. "It wasn't the *preferred* way to live; it was a survival technique that pulled people together to fix what was lacking and to change 'surviving' into 'thriving.'

"Long after women and children were able to move on from this *ad hoc* networking, they maintained friendships and contacts for many years to come.

Cecilia added, "It was deemed so effective, that single fathers started doing the same thing. It was never about dating, it was about getting together to solve the problem of single-parent childcare while one continued their education. This was not a time for romantic entanglements. The groups were laser-focused on getting certificates, licenses, and degrees so that they could enter the job market geared to support their families. It was a survival mechanism for the overwhelming cost and limited hours and limited hours of childcare. It was twenty-four-hours-a-day, seven-days-a-week *and,* most importantly, *it was free.*"

Elena nodded her head, "The 'Perfect Family' ideal never worked. It was considered to be proper and appropriate and religiously sound for the man to be head of the family, and then the wife (or wives) is subordinate and dependent on him, along with their children. If this were true then, idealy, they would live happily ever after.

"But, men die. Men leave. Men get sick. Men drink. Men abuse. Men go off to war with the real possibility of not ever returning. This leaves the woman uneducated, unable to support herself, and her children, and dependent on (and at the mercy of) the next dominate male in her life, or quite possibly destitute on the street."

Cecilia agreed.

"But," Elena continued, "if we let go of this mold, then the woman is educated, employed, involved in her own decisions about her life, and the lives of her family members, and that includes whether or not to marry or have children.

"This also takes the pressure off of a man," Cecilia added. "Having to provide, having to go to school, having to make all of the decisions for so many lives other than his own. Maybe he never even *wanted* to marry or have kids, so the idea of the 'Perfect Family' wasn't ideal for him either."

"Agreed," Elena nodded her head. "The single-parent family is not, by all means, perfect either; time, money, energy, all tremendous, even for healthy children, and that single parent could get sick, injured, unemployed, or even die."

Both ladies were quiet with introspection. Elena warmed-up each teacup with fresh brew.

Quietly, she sipped her tea and thought of the atrocities one sex did to the other. It was an overwhelmingly male-dominated category of human behavior: Sexual intimidation, sexual battery, sexual assault, sexual torture. Logically speaking, what a woman could do is more powerful than what a man could do and should be considered the more powerful sex due to their ability to create the next generation after only a little action from men. For tens of thousands of years, societies were Egalitarian, Matriarchal or Patriarchal, but, sometime before the Common Era, a switch was flipped so that muscle and testosterone-flavored aggression won over, time and again. As a long-admired lawman once asked, "Questioning society with the simple query, why?"

"Let's do some brainstorming, my friend," Elena urged.

Cecilia's focus came back to the room, "About what?"

"The horrors of the world; the ugliest words in the human language."

Cecilia was dubious, "What on Earth for?"

"Well, we are walking through a swamp here. This has got to be the most depressing conversation we've ever had. Let's brace ourselves and walk forward to the other side. Let's cleanse our souls by acknowledging what has happened. Then, when we're done, we're done, never having to come this way again."

Silence, then…

"Well," Cecilia started in, "Of the flood of images on my mind now, I can see that the worst of humanity was carved out by the male of the species. Are we really going there?"

"We're going," urged Elena. "Let's finish this."

"Human trafficking; witch hunts; invaders; marauders; human and animal sacrifices; genital mutilations; slavery; indentured servitude; child soldiers; sex traders and sex trade supporters; sex slaves; molesters; raping infants; domestic abuse; child brides; polygamy…"

Elena added, "The black-market; debt servitude; intentional ignorance; making false claims; doing nothing in the face of evil; terrorists; cyberattacks; stalkers; abandonment of responsibility; ethnic cleansings; blindly following orders; vivisections; forced starvation; incarceration of innocents; internment camps; concentration camps; prisoner-of-war camps; unauthorized governmental or industrial experiments on the public; anti-government compounds; poaching; abductions; assassinations; eugenics; state-sponsored abortions; mass killers; mass suicides; suicide bombers; hostage-taking; dictators; megalomaniacs…"

"Consistently and historically the highest echelons of authority and power in religion; maritodespotism; committing a spouse to an insane asylum or house-of-God to get out of the marriage; cannibals; serial killers; brutalized their own sex; brutalized the opposite sex; incest; 'rape-correcting' a lesbian; rapist-fathers suing their victims for custody of a baby that was conceived during the assault; using rape as a punishment to correct a woman's perceived societal transgressions; honor killings…"

"Hazing; trolling; uses terms of the opposite sex to insult those of your own sex; sex tourism; has concubines; manias; fetishes; gangs; pressganging;

debt bondage; organized crime; animal trappers; zoos; animal torture; animal experiments; animal extinctions; plant extinctions; nuclear, well, everything; crimes against humanity; human and animal sacrificing for god or spirits; forcing natives to convert to (usually) Western ideals of education, language, customs, appearance, diet, and religion; seizing natives to be sold as slaves; slave trafficking; slave auctions; slave owners; raping or abusing slaves; mass incarcerations; workhouses; sweatshops; extortion; smuggling; brutalizing children; brutalizing animals and bestiality; brutalizing the Earth…"

Cecilia continued, "Panthenophilla; parthenolatry; ghost brides; child marriages; harassment; assault; sexual harassment; sexual assault; sexual impropriety; pinching, grabbing, and groping strangers; psychological torment; rape; gang rape; marital rape or abuse not considered a crime because she's his wife, or considered his property; date rape; rape rallies; child pornographers; drugging females and children for unopposed access to their bodies; 'revenge porn;' 'stealthing'…"

"Streaming murders, rapes, tortures, abuse, hatred; exclusive and single-sexed clubs; exclusive and single-sexed schools; exclusive and single-sexed houses of worship; necromania; the greediest of corporations; warmongering; abusing power; sabotage; treason…"

"Democide…"

"Democide?" Elena interrupted.

"Ah, yes," Cecilia responded. "Similar to genocide, it's a nice, clean word for the murder of a populace by their own government. It boggles my mind that democide surpassed war, world-wide, in the 20th Century, as the *leading cause of death*. Well aside from natural death, anyway. Governments are supposed to work for the people, and protect the people. Even democratic governments pulled that shit." Cecilia delicately put her teacup down. "Add to that, genocide."

"Wow." Elena was quiet. Moments later, she took a deep breath and continued with the list of horrors. "Chemical-, biological-, and radiological-warfare; family abandonment; spousal death; abuse, abandonment or divorce for lack of a male heir; infanticide for being the 'wrong' sex; drug cartels; lynching; home invasions; spree killers; mass killers; killers for hire; mercenaries; online predators; invasion; governments overthrown; car-jacking; hijacking; train robberies; bank robberies; white-collar crimes;

blue-collar crimes; war crimes; war lords; kingpins; raids; smugglers; pirates…"

Elena took a deep breath, and then continued, "Using animals as a sacrifice; using humans, particularly virgins as a sacrifice; using girls or women, particularly virgins, as a prize or as a reward; coercion for fellatio or sex by dropping legal (or illegal) charges (or false charges); getting, or finding, someone addicted to drugs and then using their torment against them by using their bodies in a sex-for-drugs exchange; hiring one or more people out for sex, and then keeping a percentage of their earnings; infidelities outside of one's marriage; unwelcomed salacious or lecherous leering, jeering, joking, winking, whistling, taunting, 'pet' name calling, and/or being overly familiar to a person whether known or unknown to the harasser, often escalating to anger and/or sexist slurs if rebuffed which, potentially, could escalate again to uninvited close contact or sexual contact; flashing; mansplaining; manspreading…"

Cecilia closed her eyes, "Double standards; dehumanizing, marginalizing, or subjugating females in the media; dehumanizing, marginalizing, or subjugating females in entertainment; dehumanizing, marginalizing, or subjugating females in advertising; dehumanizing, marginalizing, or subjugating females in politics; dehumanizing, marginalizing, or subjugating females in the education; dehumanizing, marginalizing, or subjugating females in legislation; dehumanizing, marginalizing, or subjugating females in workforce; dehumanizing, marginalizing, or subjugating females in religion; dehumanizing, marginalizing, or subjugating females in their culture or home…"

"Um, bullying; coercion by fear, intimidation, or threats; systematically and automatically granting children to one parent in a case of divorce without considering facts that might prove this action to be faulty or dangerous to the children's welfare…"

"Yes. Ah, higher salaries and/or more opportunities in the work force than the opposite sex; intersectionality…"

"Of course," Elena nodded.

"We repeated some ideas…"

"That's ok," Elena said. "We were brainstorming.

"All of these events and actions are, far and above, perpetrated and *perpetuated* by men. Men, who have claimed for thousands of years that they are stronger, smarter, and more capable than women, and granted dominion over all by God, have laid waste to their own species, their own planet."

Cecilia added, "And even after their 'God-given' supreme command over women, over animals and over the Earth on which they roam, men have befouled it all." She took a sip of tea, returned the cup to its saucer, and then looked into her friend's eyes, "And, if you take the idea, the goal, of male gratification out of this equation, then what's left of that long list we came up with when we brainstormed the horrors of the world and the ugliest words in the human language?"

"Ohhhhhhhhh!" Elena exclaimed. "*Oh, wow! It almost completely disappears!*"

"The history of humanity," Cecilia spoke softly, "Keeps coming back to male domination with their goal being male gratification. In fact, the so-called *world's oldest profession* wouldn't exist at all if men didn't pay for sex. But, if men didn't have this option then, most likely, there would have been a lot more rapes world-wide, as well as more laws demanding female obedience and subjugation. Male gratification…"

"Compassion and empathy," Elena insisted, "aren't weaknesses; it's thinking about something or someone other than yourself! One should think that *selfishness* is weak. Looking after oneself and loving oneself is strength, but always thinking *only* of oneself above all others, well… *Non nobis solum nati sumus.*"

Cecilia sat back with her teacup in hand, "Not unto ourselves alone are we born. Interesting phrase. I think that women are the most amazing creatures on Earth."

"I agree my friend," Elena sat forward with her tea cup. "Even after all of that abuse and degradation…still, she doesn't hate men."

"Still, she serves others."

"Still, she defends her country."

"Still, she heals others or comforts them in their time of need."

"Still, she earns."

"Still, she governs."

"Still, she creates."

"Still, she rises."

CHAPTER 13

SPACETIME

In this other world, Dr. Mary Edwards Walker spoke to a full classroom. In fact, her lectures now needed to be located in the school's largest auditorium, and even then, it was standing room only.

When a bell chimed the hour, she began.

"Although the sex of a baby is decided at the moment of conception by the father's genetic donation, it's dihydrotestosterone at eight weeks that changes the previously generic embryo into a male fetus, and with the *absence* of this additional hormone the previously generic embryo develops as a female fetus.

"This happens when we are only the size of a thumbnail, before we even develop our fingerprints or skin tone. In fact, we still have just a little bit left of our caudle tail.

"Imagine that: For fifty-six days on Earth everyone one of us was created equal.

"Destinies split drastically from that point, and at fifteen weeks, the male fetus' brain is flooded with another high dose of testosterone – twice as much as the female fetus'.

"The testosterone hormone changes competitiveness, aggressiveness, risk-taking parameters, and might even change the brain structure at seventeen-weeks, making it *a male brain*. The next most notable change for each sex is puberty.

"With men," Dr. Walker spoke clearly, "It always came back to their penises, and their surprising lack of control over such a simple organ. A

71

loan maiden headed back to the kitchen gets raped by a knight headed back to the hall; a passed-out party girl gets raped by a party boy; lawlessness reigns after a disaster and groups of men wandered the streets collecting women and girls to be put to the highest bidder's use as sex slaves; a woman, discreetly covered and minding her own business, walks down a street and gets raped by a man who claims that it was her fault because she wasn't chaperoned by a man; invaders pillaged and raped; male service members raped female service members; even with same-sex incarceration gang rape was common, and men who were born heterosexual often entered into *consensual* sexual relations with fellow convicts after prolonged submersion in an all-male environment.

"Violence promoted rape. Aggression promoted rape. Lack of respect for a female promoted rape; a man's lack of self-control promoted rape. Society's indifference to, and rationalization of, rape promoted rape.

"Continuing intercourse after a previously consensual partner has changed her or his mind and wants to stop for any reason, is rape.

"Continuing intercourse with a victim who wants to stop, but has stopped struggling, is rape.

"Brutalizing a person into submission or taking advantage of someone who is not able to say 'no' is not a 'yes.' It is not consent. It is not respect. It does, however, make you a rapist; a sex offender. And, if you do it more than once, it makes you a serial rapist.

"No one 'asks' or even 'begs' to be raped; those two ideas are mutually exclusive.

"It's not a dare, it's not a prank, it's not a joke, and it's not 'boys will be boys.'

"It doesn't matter if your god says rape is ok and it doesn't matter if the devil made you do it. It doesn't matter what country you're from, it doesn't matter what religion you believe in, or if you are given absolution, it doesn't matter how old you are, it doesn't matter what you tell yourself, it doesn't matter if she or he forgives you, it doesn't matter if the law is on your side, it doesn't matter if you 'paid your debt to society': If you have sex with someone without consent then you are a rapist.

"Instead of ordering modesty, why don't you *practice* modesty? Instead of leering at a woman's cleavage, why don't you look away? Instead calling a woman a whore, why don't you avoid sexually explicit media? Instead of demanding that a woman be covered from head to toe, blotting out her features and her humanity, why don't you look her in the eye and appreciate her for who she is rather than whoever it is you want her to be?

"It is easier to push people around. It is easier to have it your way. It is easier to have less competition. It is easier to have free labor. It is easier to shut people out and to shout them down rather than having to bother with treating them with respect. Women have paid the price for Patriarchy, but they have never gained much value from it.

"There were women, though, who have bucked the system. There were women who spoke out. There were women who pushed the known parameters of their station in life to make their mark or better the lives of others. Many were killed for their efforts, and many others were lost to the oblivion of time and never recorded in history simply because of their sex, but here are some who have made it outside and into the sunshine.

"Fu Hao, the world's first known woman warrior, living about 3500 years ago during the Chinese Bronze Age, lead armies of 13,000 men into battle. When she died, she was buried with horses, slaves, chariots, and axes.

"In Mesopotamia, when Patriarchal laws were being carved into cones, Enheduanna, high-priestess of Ur, became the first literary author anywhere ever to write in the first person, identifying herself, 'I am Enheduanna.'

"In Egypt, Hatshepsut, the greatest of the female pharos, was considered to be one of the most successful and effective pharos, man or woman, to ever rule. She was a prolific builder, with many leaders after her claiming her work to be theirs. She also opened up trade with other countries by sending out five ships. Most significantly returning from foreign ports, these ships carried live trees, frankincense, and myrrh. The trees proved to be the first time anyone had ever tried to transplant trees from foreign soil and, for the first time, frankincense resin was burned and used as one of the ingredients in the classic Egyptian eyeliner. When Hatshepsut died in 1458 BCE of bone cancer from using a carcinogenic lotion, she was buried in the Valley of the Kings.

"The Scythians, in the 1st Century BCE, were Eurasian nomads, warriors, herders, and equestrians. They also had a deep understanding of metallurgy, tanning, textiles, and weapons-making. The women dressed as the men dressed, and were buried as the men were buried—with their weapons.

"In Southeast Asia, in 41 CE, Vietnam's Trung sisters, Trac and Nhi, raised 80,000 troops and lead the uprising against invasive China. They were all cut down and Vietnam came under Chinese rule for the next nine centuries but, a millennium later, many believed that if the Trung sisters had not raised the rebellion, then Vietnam wouldn't have survived at all.

"Empress Theodora and co-ruler Emperor Justinian of the Byzantine Empire later reached sainthood. But before he could even marry her, Justinian had to abolish a law which had previously made it illegal for him to marry a common woman. When they ascended to the throne in 527, he called her 'my partner in deliberations.'

"During their reign, plague, riots, and rebellion endangered the couple's very lives. Once, when Justinian prepared to flee during one such trouble, Theodora said that he could leave if he wished, and reach a safe, distant shore, living out the rest of his life in exile. But once there, wouldn't he wish that he had lived and died here, as Emperor? They stayed, fought and won the rebellion and, for the rest of his life, Justinian felt that he owed his very thrown to his wife, Empress Theodora.

"Together they rebuilt Constantinople, making it the most stunningly beautiful city in the world. Their crown jewel was the rebuilt Hagia Sophia church, an architectural wonder all on its own.

"During their reign, the empress pushed lawmaking that protected women, closed brothels, and gave rapists the death penalty.

"Justinian outlived his wife, who died in 548, mourning her passing deeply.

"A thousand years later, Granuile 'Grace' O'Malley, daughter to an Irish clan chieftain, was born around 1530. She, being born female, was just supposed to marry and have babies but, instead, she chose her own destiny, becoming one of the greatest clan warriors Ireland ever had ever seen.

"Early on, the 'Pirate Queen,' as she was to be called, wanted to go to sea with her father, but was repeatedly denied because of her gender. Deciding not to accept this as her destiny, she stowed away on her father's ship, popping out only after they were too far out to return. Acknowledging her determination, her father, the powerful chieftain, Black Oak, finally relented and took her under his wing.

"After what was most likely some fierce deliberations, a bargain must have been struck, because she could now go to sea, but it appears she also had to marry.

"She had three children by her first husband, but was widowed young, just eight years later. Upon his death, O'Malley took to sea with her husband's crew.

"She *had to be* successful as an exceptional mariner, trader, and leader or her people would not have followed her, and her adversaries wouldn't have feared her.

"Her military history was recorded by her enemies, English scribes who kept Queen Elizabeth I informed. She was an excellent swordswoman and fighter, and Clew Bay was O'Malley's territory. She knew it well, and it was there that she and her men took down the English, ship after ship.

"When her father died, she staked her claim to become chieftain, the first female to do so. O'Malley lived her life as chieftain by superbly deciding was best for herself, her family, and those of whom she led. Raiding other clan's strongholds was common in Ireland's feudal society, and O'Malley excelled at it; her clan swelled with 5000 head of cattle, 1000 horses and massive herds of sheep.

"To expand her reach, and to remain strong against the English, she married for a second time. The product of this union was her favorite son, which she gave birth to while at sea.

"During an altercation with the English, O'Malley's oldest son, Owen, and all who were with him were killed. She retaliated, but her warriors were outnumbered 25-to-1. O'Malley was captured and accused of treason against the Crown, but she could be released if her crew agreed to take her place, which they gladly did for their leader.

"After years of warfare with the English, Irish lands were burned, crews were lost, and families were pillaged. In an attempt to ease the suffering of her people, O'Malley asked for an audience with the English queen.

"It took years but, eventually, the request was granted and O'Malley arrived in Greenwich to plead her case against her clan's greatest tormentor, an Englishman named Bingham. His cruelties against her people included the murder of her own son.

"She and the queen were the same age, and it is believed that the queen admired the pirate. Queen Elizabeth granted her all that she had asked for, including recalling Bingham back to England to demand that he answer to charges of abuse of power.

"O'Malley and Queen Elizabeth both died in 1603, both were 67 years old, and both died quietly of natural causes.

"Historians wrote the Pirate Queen out of history as 'the woman who overstepped the bounds of womanhood,' but her deeds lived on in song and legend."

Dr. Walker took a sip of water.

"For over 600 years, ending in 1923, the Ottoman Empire was guided by Islam, and the greatest emperor was aptly named Sultan Suleiman *the Magnificent.*

"For a wife he chose Roxelana, who had been kidnapped from the Ukraine at age 15 and sold into sexual slavery to the harem of the Empire's government.

"Before this union, sultans were not allowed to marry, so to make new leaders sultans were bred with these palace sex slaves. A son became a sultan only after killing off all of his brothers. In this snake pit of violence, every candidate had his mother behind him to rally support; they would either rise or fall together.

"But this time, something had changed. Roxelana fell in love with Sultan Suleiman, and he with her. They broke with the hard-and-fast rules and traditions when he freed her and married her in 1534. He renamed her Hurrem, meaning 'The Laughing One,' and with her had five sons and one daughter.

"After this, generations followed the same path, fundamentally changing the family dynamics from murderous to amorous. At this time in history, the Ottoman Empire was about 20 million strong. This new type of relationship had the power to change a lot of minds and as many destinies."

Dr. Walker smiled and cleared her throat.

"In India, Persian-born Mehr-un-Nissa became Empress Nur Jahan, meaning 'Light of the World.'

"She was the twentieth and last wife of Emperor Jahangir, and she took up the reign of power as his Padshah Begum, his empress, not to try to usurp his power, but to support him.

"Because of his love for her, she became a powerful force. She had quite a struggle ahead of her, though, with many laws and customs in the way of happiness and success.

"Contemporary with her efforts, the 'Mahabharata,' deemed to be the longest poem ever written with well over a million-and-a-half words, stated about women, 'There is nothing more evil than women; a wanton woman is a blazing fire… She is poison, a serpent, and death all in one.'

"Cheerful, isn't it?

"Many agreed with the idea of toxic women. The Hindu and Islamic faiths had both adopted *purdah* (meaning 'curtain'). It's the religious and social practice of female seclusion either by a physical wall or by covering their entire bodies, concealing their form. Nur Jahan blurred these lines, by redesigning traditional clothing so that women could move easier.

"But in politics, she couldn't show her face, so she whispered to her husband from behind a screen. Despite this limitation, through him, she became so powerful that traders had to work with her and every treaty or agreement had to have her stamp of her approval.

"She's the *only* Padshah Begum to be granted so much power, and she's the *only* Padshah Begum to have a coin struck with her name. That was quite a feat for someone who's supposed to be hidden.

"She was a powerfully built woman, decisive, courageous, and smart, often going on hunting trips with her husband. An unknown poet said of her, 'Though Nur Jahan be in form a woman,/In the ranks of men she's a tiger-slayer.'

"And, while her husband was away, or too ill to attend, Nur Jahan kept the government going, squashed rebel uprisings, and moderated family feuds.

"She was the first to use white marble, lace carvings, and floral designs in architecture. Reflecting these talents, the Taj Mahal was built by her step-son for his wife (which happened to be Nur Jahan's niece).

"After Emperor Jahangir death, Nur Jahan was exiled, but lived very comfortably, dying nearly twenty years later in 1645. On her tomb, which she had built, her epitaph reads, 'On the grave of this poor stranger, let there be neither lamp nor rose. Let neither butterfly's wing burn nor nightingale sing.'

"This region of the world would again see a strong female leader, but not until 300 years had passed.

"Indira Gandhi became India's first (and, as it turns out, only) female prime minister, and after her first term in office, a fellow politician stated, 'India is Indira and Indira is India.'

"After a long life of service in the political arena, Gandhi's dedication to her country ended in 1984 with a bloody assassination; she was betrayed by her own bodyguards.

"The day before her murder she stated in a speech, 'I am alive today; I may not be here tomorrow... I shall continue to serve until my last breath and when I die, I can say, that every drop of my blood will invigorate India and strengthen it.'

"She went on to say, 'Even if I died in the service of the nation, I would be proud of it. Every drop of my blood... will contribute to the growth of this nation and to make it strong and dynamic.'

"Famously, in 1999, Indian Prime Minister Indira Priyadarshini Gandhi was internationally rewarded when she was named, 'Woman of the Millennium,' by a British television news network known as the 'BBC.'

"And that's even after Albanian-born Anjezë Gonxhe Bojaxhiu, better known as Mother Teresa, started in India, in 1950, the Missionaries of Charity, who would serve 'the hungry, the naked, the homeless, the crippled, the blind, the lepers, all those people who feel unwanted, unloved, uncared for throughout society, people that have become a burden to the society and are shunned by everyone.'

"That charity spread worldwide and, for 50 years, Mother Teresa served India, dying in Calcutta, as a citizen of India, in 1997, at age 87.

"During her life, she was awarded the Nobel Peace Prize, and after her death she was canonized as a Roman Catholic saint.

"Not to take anything away from Indira Gandhi's success, but..." Dr. Walker shook her head, "Perhaps Mother Teresa came in second place in the contest for the 'Woman of the Millennium' award."

Dr. Walker paused for a moment, then shook her head again, "Let's take a ten minute break."

She stepped away from the podium and took a moment to refresh herself with a few sips of water. No one else had moved.

"Feel free to move about. Stretch yourself. Take a bathroom break. We'll begin again upon your return."

The crowd remained seated, quiet, and in rapt attention.

"Shall we continue, then?"

Over 300 gleeful assents sounded out.

"Wow. Ok, then." She smiled, cleared her throat, and returned to the podium.

"China's Wang Cong'er was born in 1777. Her father died when she was a child, and her mother raised her by herself. Begging on the streets for food to survive, she lived among the results of a corrupt rule.

"Wang took up with a troupe of entertainers and learned social skills and martial arts in the eight years among them. She became an expert in the spiritual enlightenment, fitness and weapons of kung-fu. This was extremely rare for women, and her achievements gave her the respect of men.

"At sixteen, she was attacked by a group of men that she couldn't fight off by herself. The man who intervened, Chi Lin, was an underground leader and fighter against the corrupted Chinese rule. He was also her future husband.

"Together they headed the White Lotus Society and planned a rebellion against the emperor. Among other things, the Society promoted an Egalitarian philosophy, making it highly attractive to women.

"During this time, the population doubled to about 350 million people, with no corresponding changes in food availabilities, or living conditions.

"In 1794, the uprising began. The army, clued-in by a White Lotus Society traitor, was on high alert and, during a festival, Chi Lin and hundreds of his fellow rebels fell into a trap and were executed.

"Mulan, as Wang Cong'er was then known, was grief stricken, and the leaderless movement was adrift.

"It wasn't long, though, before she decided to take up the fight; she began training 20,000 warriors.

"Mulan was a unique fighter. She fought with a sword in each hand, both on the ground and on horseback.

"This new skill of riding on horseback using only legs and feet continued to be taught in China for hundreds of years. The horses in this peasant army were hardy, well-trained, and learned to obey signals from knees, feet, as well as voice commands that could get the horses to rear-up to fight with hooves, or even to bite.

"As fighting intensified, Mulan linked up with the leaders of five other peasant provinces for a force of 100,000 troops. She favored a surprise attack while the others wanted a more cautious route.

"In March, 1798, she split from the group and led her 20,000 to fight the 100,000 Ch'ing forces alone. This was a fatal mistake. Her army was slaughtered after only six hours of fighting, leaving Mulan, and a handful of survivors, surrounded.

"At only twenty-two years of age, Mulan chose to join her husband in death by, reportedly, throwing herself off a cliff. Their fight was over.

"Many years later it was said that, 'the deadliest of all the rebels are those led by Madam Wang, wife of Qi.'"

Dr. Walker paused to clear her throat before continuing.

"Great women were not systematically recorded in history; only the men counted. Engraved on the great Panthéon of Paris, finished in 1790, it said 'To great men, a grateful nation.' All of the French heroes of the 18th and 19th Centuries were honored there, but not a single woman.

"And, even into the 21st Century, seventy-one men made it into those hallowed halls, but only four women. The first, Sophie Berthelot was merely buried with her husband, Marcellin Berthelot, a chemist whose principle about affinity was later disproved.

"Maria Salomea Skłodowska-Curie was also buried with her husband, Pierre Curie, but Madame Curie (who died in 1934) was the first to be buried in the Panthéon on her own merit.

"Among her other accomplishments, she is the only *PERSON* in the world to have earned a Nobel Prize in two different disciplines: Physics *and* Chemistry. Memorably, she is noted as saying during World War I, 'I am going to give up the little gold I possess (for the cause). I shall add to this the scientific medals, which are quite useless to me.'

"The Curies were enshrined in the Panthéon in 1995.

"Geneviève de Gaulle-Anthonioz (who died in 2002) and Germaine Tillion (who died in 2008) were both symbolically interred in 2015 with coffins containing nothing but soil from their gravesites, per their family's request. They were both apart of the French Resistance during World War II.

"Four French women honored. *Four*.

"The legendary Joan of Arc was insignificantly born as a French peasant's daughter in 1412, but she died just nineteen years later, burned at the stake in the hands of the English, as a general, and a patriot. Later, she would be declared a martyr and a she would even eventually become a saint! One would think that her name would grace the Panthéon but oddly, more memorials of her could be found in *England* than in *France*.

"The historic storming of Versailles in 1789, an early rebellion in the French Revolution, was led by women; it was even known as, 'The Women's March of Versailles.' This crowd of thousands wanted, among other things, a constitutional monarchy with the power shifting from the king to the people. This resistance started a war that lasted nearly ten years.

"'The Declaration of the Rights of Man and of the Citizen' became the keystone, the *foundation*, of France's new government.

"Written in 1789, the same year as the women's march, it mimics the Constitution of the United States and its Bill of Rights. And it, along with the Magna Carta and other historic papers influenced, 160 years later, the writing of the 'United Nations Universal Declaration of *Human* Rights,' in 1948.

"For this to happen, imagine just how visionary, how powerful, and how water-tight that French document had to be! Still, it fell short as it only regarded and protected the rights of men and their property. 'Active citizens,' as they were called, were considered property-owning men, and they had the right to vote and held the power. 'Passive citizens' included women, children, slaves, men without property, and foreigners; no property, no power, no vote, no rights.

"Olympe de Gouges countered this narrow thinking by writing, in 1791, 'The Declaration of Women and the Female Citizen,' It was seen almost as a political satire compared to the legal document it was based on. Article I of 'The Declaration of the Rights of Man and of the Citizen' stated, 'Men are born and remain free and equal in rights. Social distinctions may be based only on common utility.' Whereas, Article I of 'Declaration of the Rights of Woman and the Female Citizen' responded with 'A woman is born free and remains equal to man in rights. Social distinctions may only be based on common utility.'

"In the Age of Enlightenment, when reason should have won over superstition, philosopher Jean-Jacques Rousseau, whose writings helped encourage the revolution, wrote, 'Man should be strong and active, the woman should be weak and passive.' And to this, Olympe de Gouges countered with her '*Contrat Social*'; her Social Contract argued that women should be regarded equally in marriage.

"She believed also that women should be lawyers and ambassadors, and be in politics, and have children outside of marriage. She wanted a debate, but it wasn't even put on the agenda. After the 'Reign of Terror' began in France, the government took extreme measures like banning women from meeting in groups of five or more for fear of yet another uprising.

"De Gouges went on to encourage the public to defend themselves, and for this, she was arrested, tried, sentenced and put to death by guillotine. This was only the beginning of a political backlash against French women.

"Olympe de Gouges was *the only woman* to state, on paper, that the 'Rights of Man' didn't include the 'Rights of Woman.' She should have been honored in the Panthéon. And while 20th Century protesters wanted the Panthéon to reflect the *actual* heroes of France, that nation was slow to correct its historical errors.

"The post-revolution Napoléonic Code, which went into effect in 1804, was a disaster for women's rights giving their fathers and husbands absolute power over them. There wasn't much hope for women when Emperor-King-Protector-Mediator-Co-Prince-Sovereign Napoléon Bonaparte himself believed that, 'Women ought to obey us. *Nature has made women our slaves!*'

"Not until 1946 could French women vote, and it took another twenty years for them to be able to work outside of the home without their husband's permission. *Truly unbelievable!*

"What made it even worse was that the Code influenced European lawmaking during and after the Napoléonic Wars, and even found its way into the Middle East. Some saw Napoléon as a military genius, while others saw him only as a tyrant, but the fact is that his heavy-handed laws against women traveled far and wide affecting millions for hundreds of years."

Dr. Walker paused in a moment of respect for the down-trodden before continuing.

"The Apache's Lozen, of the American West's Indian Warm Springs Apache tribe was born around 1840. She fought with Geronimo and Victorio in the Indian Wars against the U.S. Army's manifest destiny. She was a warrior, a seer, and a medicine woman, making her indispensable on the warpath.

"Victorio said that his little sister was as powerful as any other warrior, yet as a woman, her story was not recorded in anything but the traditional sense.

"After years of war, Chief Victorio wanted peace for his people. He would eventually concede the entire area known as Apacheria in exchange for a much smaller parcel of land and a promise of peace. But this was not to be.

"Again, only wanting peace, the much smaller territory known as Ojo Calienta became the Apache home, by treaty, but even this was not honored by the U.S. Calvary who invaded and attacked the settlement. Victorio's family and many others were massacred.

"Other leaders, including Geronimo, were harassed by soldiers. Again, to maintain peace, Victorio surrendered to the U.S. Army's General Hatch. Hatch urged Washington to uphold the treaty and return the Apaches to their promised land, but instead, the Apache were run off to open their present location up to mining.

"Clear now that they would never be left alone, Lozen and Victorio decided to go to war. Lozen was the master of guerilla warfare. She knew the terrain and tricked the Army again and again, leaving them without horses, guns, ammunition, or out in the desert without water.

"Lozen put herself in danger for her people, and her tactics again and again, kept them safe while the opposite side lost troops. This earned her the respect of her people.

"Evading and attacking the Army that was reinforced with Buffalo Soldiers, the Apache had the upper hand in Black Range.

"General Hatch started recruiting Apache scouts from the reservation in Arizona to track Lozen down.

"In 1880, the warriors of Apache tribes Chiricahua and Mescalero ambushed two companies of Calvary who were, in fact, trying to ambush them. The only thing that saved the army was reinforcements the very next morning.

"Constantly on the run, the Apaches became exhausted and wounded. They headed south, but as they crossed into Mexico, Mexican forces attacked, killing many including Victorio. Only seventeen out of four hundred survived.

"Five years later, Lozen joined up with Geronimo seeking revenge. It was 5000 troops versus only a few scores of Apache most of whom were women and children.

"Making camp deep into Mexico, they knew that they had only two choices: They could become prisoners, in prison camps in Florida or die.

"Again, thinking of the survival of their tribe, Geronimo surrendered in September 1886. The promise was two years imprisonment with their families, and then they'd be allowed to return to their homelands.

"This turned into *twenty-eight* years in St. Augustine, Florida. After which, they were moved to Alabama where they were all exposed to tuberculosis and died. They were never given the change to return to their homelands, and the mines they were run off of were eventually abandoned so, sadly, there was no need to ever hunt anybody down, or run anybody off. They could have stayed there and lived in peace had the United States government kept their word."

Dr. Walker paused, to let that sink in.

"In some places, like South Africa, women fought alongside men for freedom, but in too many other places, women were nothing more than chattel, wombs, or concubines.

"At the beginning of the 19th Century, the only hope for English girls was to stay at home until they married, but Millicent Garrett Fawcett couldn't understand why women should have any less of an education, or be kept from politics.

"She also fought to criminalize child abuse and incest, prevent child marriages, and protect a woman's right to be in the courtroom if she was charging a man with a sexual offense against her.

"Oh, and voting rights, of course. Millicent Fawcett is most remembered as being a pioneer in women's suffrage. She felt that there should be a series of lectures at Cambridge, but so many women came, that a hall had to be provided for their lodging, and opportunities for a woman to be educated at Cambridge grew from there.

"She believed in empowering women first through education, and then through legal representation. She felt that women could no longer be treated either socially or legally as if they were helpless children. But she didn't just say this; she gave them to tools to achieve these goals themselves. Fawcett campaigned from 1866 to 1928 for women's suffrage, dying at home, age 82, in 1929.

"Another Englishwoman, Emily Wilding Davison fought for women's suffrage using other tactics. She used shouts and interruptions, violence and arson.

"Arrested nine times, she and others went on hunger-strikes in prison. These were countered with prison officials force-feeding the protesters by violently shoving tubes up their noses and down their throats.

"Undeterred in her iron resolve to lift women up from their powerless lives, Ms. Davison was force-fed forty-nine times. She died slowly, but not in prison, and not from starvation.

"On a fine June day in 1913, she intentionally stepped out onto a racetrack, right in front of King George V's own horse who was running at top speed. She died of her injuries four excruciating days later.

"Tens-of-thousands of people lined the streets of London to watch thousands of suffragettes attend to her coffin as it left the city for burial in Northumberland.

"She had, quite literally, sacrificed her own body for the cause. The horse and jockey were fine, if that's where your concerns lie; both raced two weeks later.

"Although it's unlikely that Davison spotted and specifically targeted the king's horse, her luck at being struck by him garnered more attention then had it been any other horse.

"Many were angry at the disruption of the sport, while others rallied for the cause resulting in men forming the group 'Northern Men's Federation for Women's Suffrage.'

"England wasn't the only one reluctant to give women the right to vote; 1928, for them. Norway didn't allow such a thing until 1913 and Denmark in 1915. The first ever to allow women to vote was New Zealand in 1893, although not even a country until 1907. For that honor, I give you Finland in 1906! It was the first country to ever adopt *universal* suffrage, and they followed-up that magnificent law with action: The following year, Finland elected the world's first female members of parliament. Outstanding achievements!"

Dr. Walker beamed.

"In Eastern Europe," she continued, "Russia's Alexandra Kollontai was the first woman to enter the inner circle of the Bolshevik government, but her name is not seen among the revolutionaries.

"She spoke four languages and wanted to further her studies at the university, but her mother denied her of this, stating that she only needed to get a teacher's certificate and a husband. Period. End of story.

"Kollontai story didn't end there, though. She did marry, but later left him to fight for women's equality after seeing the conditions in a factory her husband was about to manage.

"She believed that there was a mutual need, and therefore should be a mutual respect and mutual equality. She was exiled in 1908 for her efforts.

"On International Women's Day in 1917, women organized strikes and poured into the streets. Then, in quick succession, the Tsar fell from power, Vladimir Lenin becomes premier, and she returned to Russia at the beginning of the Russian Revolution. Lenin awarded Kollontai for her efforts to improve the lives of women and made her the head of a department devoted to improving the lives of women, the Zhenotdel.

"For the next eleven years the women of Zhenotdel worked within the Bolsheviks, which later became known as the Communist Party. Kollontai persuaded them to listen to her and advance women's rights. Due of the spread of the Communist Party across the globe, she promoted change in the lives of tens-of-millions of people.

"Kollontai worked to reverse illiteracy and, for the first time ever, abortions were legal.

"When Communism spread to Asia, the Zhenotdel worked hard to educate Muslim women; a first for that region. They also tried to force Muslim women to unveil, but this went too far and, most likely, reversed many of their positive efforts in the fight for equality.

"Back at home, Soviet women were pushed out of the home by propaganda because the government needed the workforce for Communism to work. Posters were put up showing women working in factories and happy to be supporting society as opposed to cooking in the home supporting only their families. The economy flourished because women effectively doubled the workforce.

"Kollontai pushed further to free women from marriage and children, but this was too much, and Lenin exiled her.

"She wrote that, 'Sexuality is a human instinct as natural as hunger or thirst.' She decried the traditional family group and felt that the Communism state would take care of the children while the parents worked for society. As cold as this sounds, she also said, 'Communist society will take upon itself all the duties involved in the education of the child, but the joys of parenthood will not be taken away from those who are capable of appreciating them.'

"As far as Russian women got, and whatever level of equality they had to men, all victories became absolutely worthless when Soviet leader Joseph Stalin reversed all rights to women in the 1940s. When a country is in crises, one of the first things to go is women's rights. *Remember that.*

"In America, social activist, abolitionist, and suffragist, Susan Brownell Anthony worked hard to, 'Organize, agitate, educate,' and insisted that this, 'must be our war cry.'

"As so many women in politics were to discover, male politicians were more concerned about a female politician's appearance than her ideas, often derisively commenting on a woman's marital status, age, hair, weight, and in Anthony's case, her shorter dress. Feeling that it took the focus off of her powerful speeches, she gave up the knee-length frocks and pantaloons and returned to wearing the heavy, floor-length, and older-fashioned dresses.

"In 1851, Anthony met her soon-to-be life-long friend and fellow social reformer, Elizabeth Cady Stanton. As Stanton's husband said of them, 'Susan stirred the puddings, Elizabeth stirred up Susan, and then Susan stirs up the world!' But Stanton herself simply stated, 'I forged the thunderbolts, she fired them.'

"On November 18, 1872, Anthony was arrested with others for attempting to vote. During her famous trial she said, 'this high-handed outrage upon my citizen's rights... you have trampled underfoot every vital principle of our government. My natural rights, my civil rights, my political rights, my judicial rights, are all alike ignored.'

"She lost the case and was fined $100 USD, but she, with the nation watching, absolutely refused to pay it.

"The judge, in turn, chose not to imprison her for the fear that she would appeal. This effectively closed the case.

"Suffragettes pushed further but lost again through the court system when, in 1875, the U.S Supreme Court ruled unanimously in *Minor v. Happersett* that 'the Constitution of the United States does not confer the right of suffrage upon anyone.'

"The only road left was to push for a Constitutional amendment. And, what a long road *that* would be."

Dr. Walker shook her head again, "It took forty-one years. But in the end, the suffragettes were greatly rewarded for their efforts: In 1920, the U.S. Constitution's 19th Amendment allowing women the universal right to vote became law.

"Fifty-nine years later, Susan B. Anthony was the first real woman to be on an American coinage. It was a dollar coin that was so small that it was often confused with the much less valuable quarter coin. Perhaps because of this, it was only made for three years and then again, commemoratively, in 1999.

"Also in 1999, a second woman was honored on a dollar coin; Sacagawea, the invaluable Indian guide on Lewis and Clark's Corps of Discovery Expedition. This coin wasn't produced for very long, either.

"Other women were honored briefly, or just on the back of state quarters, but nothing with sustained, unique, nationally circulated U.S. currency. Even the $20 bill's Harriet Tubman had to be shared with its original honoree, Andrew Jackson."

Dr. Walker's clicked her tongue in dismay.

"Women have been disregarded for far too long. Many sane women, after being abandoned by their husbands to insane asylums, and permanently separated from their children, their homes, their houses of worship, and their friends, would do what comes naturally to someone in this situation; they would act out, yelling about how they shouldn't be there. They'd cry uncontrollably, be severely depressed, and strike anyone who came near them. This event successfully got her husband out of the marriage so he could move on to greener pastures, but for her, it brought loss of freedom, abuse, drugs, isolation, electroshock therapy, and in far too many cases to count, lobotomies. This was a death sentence to untold numbers of powerless women.

"In America, Margaret Sanger was one of eleven children. Seeing the toll of multiple pregnancies on her mother's body and the family's finances, she made it her life's mission to fight for contraception. She coined the term, 'birth control' in 1914.

"Sanger saw birth control as a way for the poor to get out of poverty. Her pamphlet read, 'Mothers, can you afford to have a large family? Do you want any more children? If not, why do you have them? DO NOT KILL, DO NOT TAKE A LIFE, BUT PREVENT. Safe, Harmless information can be obtained of trained nurses at 46 Amboy St.'

"She thought that women would be healthier if they could decide if and when they wanted to have children, and that this, in turn, would bring about a healthier society.

"Contraception would also put an end to dangerous and deadly illegal back-alley abortions. Decades later, people would oppose Sanger and her ideas by incorrectly attributing clinical abortions to her. She died in 1966, and the first legal abortions in the United States began in 1970. And, again, legalizing contraception, making it available to even the poorest of the public and teaching sex education would *drastically reduce* the number of abortions, unwanted pregnancies, and neglected, abused, or abandoned children. Quite simply: More children would be born to love and kindness, *simply because they were wanted.*

"To further Sanger's lifework, heiress Kathrine McCormick gifted $1,000,000 to fund the research for the world's first contraceptive medication. The Pill, as it was called, was the idea of a woman, for women, funded by a woman with no government funds – all with the goal to liberate women. On May 9th, 1960, the Pill was finally federally approved, and Sanger lived long enough to see it happen.

"Her unfortunate work in eugenics was used to smear and discredit her name by men, by conservatives, and by governments who rejected using government funds to support Planned Parenthood's legal abortions even though government funds were not used for this purpose.

"Because of this bit of misinformation, the 21st Century saw massive defunding for Planned Parenthood, the very organization that Sanger started. A hundred years of working to educate men, women, and children as well as offering affordable healthcare to those in need was directly threatened by those who didn't need sex education or free annual exams. It was shameful and deeply disturbing."

Dr. Walker paused and shook her head in despair.

"The first wave of feminism succeeded in winning the right to vote, but it didn't win a spot for women at the tables of power.

"The second wave of feminism began in the 1960s with women now being able to maintain careers in the workforce without being interrupted or sidelined with an unexpected pregnancy. This second wave was focused not just on reproductive rights, but also advanced education, equality in the workforce, and a woman's right to her own body as well as her right to live outside of the family-group paradigm. Like tsunami waves, feminism wasn't one-and-done; the waves just kept coming.

"This movement was both delayed and promoted by the Second World War. During the war, women discovered they could earn their own money when they were called on to work in the factories and shipyards for the sake of the war. But, when the war ended in 1945, those women were instructed to leave the workforce and return home, marry, and have children.

"Despite being the most powerful country on Earth, after decades of effort and new laws supporting equal opportunity in the workforce and criminalizing domestic violence, sexual harassment and sexual assault, American women continued to earn less than men, were less respected than men, were offered fewer opportunities than men and were often blamed for being sexually attacked. The U.S. was also the only industrialized country *in the world* to not have mandatory paid maternity leave. Those are signs of a weak society, don't you think?

"And, although U.S. military was once the largest in the world, it took forever for women to attain flag rank. Finally, women succeeded *and then exceeded.*

"In 2014, in the U.S. Navy's 230+ year history a woman was promoted to four-star admiral: Michelle J. Howard earned the honors. That same day, she also became VCNO, the Vice Chief of Naval Operations, making her the second-highest ranking officer in the Navy.

"Six years earlier, the Army promoted the U.S. military's very first female four-star officer, Gen. Ann E. Dunwoody.

"And in 2012, the Air Force promoted its first female four-star officer: Janet C. Wolfenbarger. Decades earlier, she was also a member of the Air Force Academy's first co-education class.

"Carol A. Mutter was the first woman in the U.S. Armed Forces to be awarded three stars, but having retired, no woman ever attained four stars in the Marines.

"Vice Admiral Jody A. Breckenridge was the highest ranking female in the U.S. Coast Guard, at least as far as my research tells me. Fantastic achievements, all! But, again, only three stars.

"On the other side of the world, in a movement called the Arab Spring, women protested against tyranny and corruption, women-exclusion and oppression. They were regularly intimidated, threatened and silenced throughout the Middle East. The good news is that that was just the first wave."

"Ok, that brings us well into the 21st Century. Let's stop there. The women of the world didn't stop there, but we will. Class dismissed."

The entire auditorium, which had remained silent and breathless for the lecture, came to their feet for a rousing standing ovation. Dr. Walker knew that it wasn't for her, it was for the women. The women.

She smiled, nodded, and added her own applause.

The women!

CHAPTER 14

CASTIGAT RIDENDO MORES

In this other world, a man named Tony Porter asked, "If it would destroy a twelve year old boy to be called a girl, what are we teaching him about girls?"

~~~

Milgram's basement office offered no windows, no way to tell what the true hour was, nor even the season. It was quite timeless.

His work was very important, none the less. He was charged with discovering why people, throughout history, did what they did, even if logic and common decency urged them to do otherwise.

People used to be far less ubuntu than they were in his time; Milgram wanted to know why.

He was working on an in-depth report that spanned millennia, but this week, he was focused on the paradigm between men and women.

There was so much data to sift through, so many sources, but for now, he just ruminated.

"Possibly, the split between men and women started at the very beginning of humanity, hundreds of thousands of years ago.

"These early humans differed from Neanderthals in that, to achieve their more extensive diet, they required a division of labor. Think of the idea of hunters and gatherers," Milgram told himself.

"These two tasks were divided not just by gender, but also by age. The men were the hunters; the women were the gatherers. But, when the men went hunting, staying behind with the women of all ages were the (weakened) aged hunters, the (weakened) injured hunters, and the (defenseless) children.

"This may have been the first smear against the respect, status, and intrinsic importance of women in the community, especially if the hunters left behind were taunted or mocked about staying back with the women by the able-bodied men off to risk their lives.

"The lessened, weakened men had lost their high status, their viability, as great hunters and providers, and now when the hunting parties headed out, they stayed back with the sick, the injured, the children, and the women. They were now *substandard* males, and their degraded status now equal to what a female's had been. This toppled female equality. From then on, females were no longer equal to men, but instead had the same dependent status as weak, defenseless, immature children. Even the most robust woman now ranked below sick, injured and even old men.

"But again, that was hundreds-of-thousands of years ago. The gender apartheid and degradation of women only continued because it had proven, time and again, to be a useful ploy of men.

"It was so strange, because women usually outlived the men in their family-groups. Why not educate them, and give them a say as to what goes on in their own lives, and in their family's lives?

"Wouldn't carrying the burden of a bunch of 'substandard' humans be detrimental to survival? Wouldn't it be logical to have as many family members as smart, and as fit as possible, so that the family-group would be able to survive hard times? The same logic follows for communities and countries, so why didn't this happen?

"Even into the 21st Century, women from the most powerful country on Earth were held back because they were considered less than men. That country was just kicking its own ass; women in the workforce, had they been paid on par with men, would have added trillions of dollars to the economy.

"In television, during this same era, strong, adult women began to headline popular, mainstream shows, but so many of them had 'girls' in the show's title. Whether they were lost, new, super, boss, or gossip, these women were in their twenties, thirties, or even in their forties, but still packaged and advertised as 'girls.'

"Contemporary memes on the internet said things along the lines of, 'A good girl is an investment; a bad one is a bill,' and, 'Don't buy that girl a drink. Buy her a taco. Girls deserve tacos.' They sounded good to most people, but the first one is quite horrible. And, as for the second one, if she's old enough to drink alcohol, she is no longer a girl; she's a woman. Again, women were degraded to child status, and judged based on their behavior rather than their intellect. Add to that, the binary thinking still graded females either as angelic or the cause of the fall.

"Incredulously, in a time when women flew commercial airliners, rescue helicopters, private airplanes and military fighter jets, a blockbuster science-fiction movie was made where inter-galactic space travel was a common, everyday thing, but it was not believed by the main characters that a 'girl,' as she was called throughout the film (even though the actress was in her twenties and the same age at her companion who was not called 'boy') could *not possibly* be a pilot.

"In fact, aside from being able to fly, she could also fix what was broken. She was mature, smart, capable, fearless, and self-sufficient. She understood at least four languages, and had a mind so powerful that the bad guy couldn't penetrate it, but she could penetrate his. This character inspired leadership and loyalty. She was untrained but incredibly powerful; a rebel, a fighter, and a defender. The movie ends with her taking over the controls of a legendary spaceship. But, you know, still a 'girl.'

"A version of a rather old board game was made based on this movie, and although she was the main character and driving force of the story, four male characters were honored with game piece tokens, and one of them wasn't even in the movie! No females were represented. Not one.

"Aside from the 'girl' there was a princess-general who was the sister of one of the represented game pieces and in the fight to defeat evil for just as long. She had more responsibility, more accountability, more scenes, more lines, and suffered more loss than her twin in this movie, but no game piece.

"There was even a female doctor who tended to one of our hero characters; no token.

"On the side of evil, there was the captain of the troops from whom one of our heroes defects and later overthrows. She, along with two of the movie characters who *were* represented by game tokens, slaughtered untold numbers of innocents, but she was not represented here.

"And then there was my favorite; a hero alien proprietor whose establishment had stood for over a thousand years.

"None of them were worth a little piece of molded token. I find this shameful, and I would bet that Elizabeth Magie would agree with me. She'd probably say something like, 'Well, that fucking figures. Patriarchy past, present, and future: Even the people who agree, and have the power to change it, don't bother changing it.'

"Not surprisingly, many of this movie studio's female animated main characters were princesses or other subservient types who'd found their men by the end of the story. Also, their mothers were usually dead or killed off early, leaving the only other descriptive option for most female characters in these movies: Evil.

"And, in that same era of science-fiction movie-making, another blockbuster was made with a predictable Patriarchal couple.

"Its leading male character was a former U.S. Navy SEAL hired by the animal park to train a group of towering vicious and deadly female carnivorous dinosaurs to obey his every command, and he succeeded in doing so because he was 'the alpha.'

"The leading female character in this movie was a happy, competent (until she lost the park), tightly-wound, well organized, by-the-numbers, top animal park executive, who had the audacity to choose career over family (as did the leading man, but this was never pointed out) who managed to pursue an escaped, pissed-off, mega-dinosaur through the hot, muddy jungle in white, three-inch high heels, and an all-white, tropical-weight, dry-clean only, high-end, skirt and blouse ensemble that managed to remain white and intact, even after hours of continuous hot pursuit through trees, wildlife trails, animal paddocks, riversides, and squatting against an abandoned jeep in a filthy garage as the roof caved in.

"Her pristine day ended with her walking down the aisle (park guests on either side) with her leading man after they proclaimed to each other that they would stick together.

"Could they have made her less stereotypically virginal? Or, could they have made her less of a stereotypically female corporate, ice queen, ball-buster? Of course they could have. But the preferred female character, even in fiction and fairytales, is a subservient and virginal 'girl' who has no business in, and poses no threat to, the male-dominated corporate world.

"Or, for that matter, the galaxy."

CHAPTER 15

ICARUS

After the well-loved public figure Icarus died, his journals were found and published. And in them, it was soon discovered that his outward views of humans-first didn't match his true thoughts or feelings about where he felt humans stood in the world…

"Humans aren't the pinnacle of life that we were led to believe. Yes, a man has a penis, but a millipede has four. Yes, humans have opposable thumbs, but koalas have two. Yes, humans have speech, dialects, language skills, and cultures, but so do countless other animals.

"Like humans, some other animals use plants for medicinal purposes and some even know how to get stoned. Some animals go to war, murder, kidnap, rape, raid, ransom, cannibalize and engage in necrophilia. Some animals become enraged, and some seek revenge. Some animals have slaves. Some animals burgle, steal, squat, and hijack another's home. Some are soldiers, some are workers, some are guards, and some are assassins.

"We are not the only ones who carry our wounded off of the battlefield. There are sadists, and there are narcissists. Many animals sing, and some create songs. Some animals farm. Some animals set traps for their prey. Some animals dream and some animals dance. Some decorate themselves. Some animals are even self-aware.

"Like humans, other animals prey on the young, the weak, the elderly, and the injured. Animals lie to protect themselves. Animals deceive with camouflage, and imitation. Some animals use tools. Most animals alter their surroundings to suit themselves, and like humans, many can use building materials and some even decorate their homes. Some animals build cities for other animals. Some can be taught the concept of money.

"For many creatures, planning ahead to avoid starvation and death is just as critical as it is for humans. Most plants and animals prepare for the changing seasons. Animals migrate, immigrate and are refugees of fires, floods, drought, disease and mass-death. Some animals adopt others, even if not of the same species, and there are many cases of non-human interspecies collaboration. And, like humans, some other animals are transgendered or even multigendered.

"Conversely, there are so many things that other animals can do, that humans can't. They can't swim to the bottom of the ocean, spin silk, hibernate, regrow limbs, echolocate, have a 360-degree field of vision, live on a hydrothermal vent, lift thirty-times their bodyweight, experience virgin births, or fly. Many insects, birds, and mammals have advanced navigational abilities without the need of technology. There are even creatures that glow in the dark.

"A tardigrade is more versatile than a human being will ever be, so if one thinks that humans are the most capable animal on Earth, meet the true apex; although not an extremophile, these magnificent creatures put humanity's self-serving pride to shame.

"For starters, they can go without food for thirty days, or water until their tiny bodies dehydrate, leaving them with only three percent moisture, and then rehydrate again with no harmful effect to the animal.

"They can be found in the deepest oceans, the highest mountain peaks, in deserts, in jungles, from pole-to-pole, and around the equator.

"Not impressed yet? They can survive temperatures near absolute zero! What naked human could withstand -272 °C? At the other end of the spectrum, tardigrades can survive the heat of 150 °C. Humans die if their own fever reaches 41 °C!

"These creatures, also known as *water bears*, can withstand pressures more than five times greater than what was experienced by the three humans briefly visiting the bottom of the deepest depths of the ocean, but those men were in grave danger and only survived encased in submersibles.

"The tardigrade's known history goes back five-hundred-and-thirty million years, and they have flourished into more than a thousand species. They have already survived meteor impacts, and it's surmised that they could even live through a supernova. The scientific community believes tardigrades will be around for another ten billion years.

"These *pudgy wudgies* can survive radiation hundreds of times higher than what would kill puny humans. And, while humanity travels around in clunky spaceships, these half-millimeter *space bears* can survive in the vacuum of space.

"Tardigrades are moss and lichen eaters, and find small invertebrates tasty, but they have never destroyed ecosystems, annihilated any species, or harmed the Earth in any way, shape, or form.

"Their omnivorous diet matches ours, putting each of us in the middle of the food chain, not at the top as so many boast. The top of the food chain, where we have long stated ourselves to be, is strictly for carnivores. Humans are no match for history's terror birds, megalodon sharks, or dinosaurs like the Spinosaurus. In fact, on the food-chain scale, humans are on par with, well, the goldfish.

"Yes, humans are currently the dominate species on Earth, but it hasn't always been so. Before us, it was something else, and after us, it will, again, be something else.

"Somehow, despite all of this, humans still claim the crown, considering themselves to be the highest form of life on Earth.

"Oh, how the mighty have fallen."

CHAPTER 16

UNNATURAL WORLD

"El-Auria?"

"I'm listening, Rachel."

"I've been studying 21st Century zoological pathology, and it's so disturbing that I'm thinking about changing subjects."

"Explain."

"We used to worry about sodium intake and cigarettes, but things were about to get so much worse. We never found the cure for cancer, no matter how many ribbons were worn. We wanted the cure for cancer, but paid no heed to the *cause*. Even after hundreds-of-billions of dollars were spent on research for the cure, we ended up with more manifestations, not less, and they were deadlier than ever before. Babies were born with cancer that soon metastasized and killed the child as a toddler. When it should have been learning the finer points of walking, feeding, toileting, and talking, it was laid to rest, pain-free at last."

"That is disturbing."

"Animals were tortured and sacrificed only to come up with drugs that cost more than most people made in a year. So, the animals suffered, and the cancer-fighters and their families were put through hell with side effects and financial ruin for absolutely worthless drugs.

"The only winners, every time, were the drug companies who spent more money on *advertising* than they did on *research*. That says it all, right there. And, while many drugs sent cancers into remission before, the majority of new treatments in the 21st Century were not effective. Eventually, that didn't matter anymore because antibiotic-resistant bacteria became deadlier than any cancer or even heart disease ever could…"

Rachel took a moment to breathe before continuing.

"Once antibiotics became obsolete, the beef industry collapsed due to consumer fears that they would contract salmonella or other bacteria from infected meat. The same thing happened with pigs, sheep, and goats. Fish and fowl industries were already destroyed, or they would have dried-up, too.

"And despite robotics performing more surgeries than humans, the chances of bacterial infections were too great, so there were no more major surgeries, organ transplants, or cancer treatments.

"Over a thousand different types of bacteria live in the human body, and DNA could not exist without viruses, but a human's life is weak and fragile especially considering that a microscopic colony of invaders could take it out.

"It became a brand new *annus terribilis*, or more realistically, an era of *anni terribilis*. Childbirth became dangerous, once again, as did childhood. Companion pets were problematic. Strep and staph infections and tuberculosis could be survived, of course, but recovery took much longer without antibiotics, and their quality of life became drastically reduced.

"Car crashes, burn victims, casualties of war all had to recover without the use of antibiotics, just as we do now, but the world's population was as stunned by this new reality as they were when the miracle drug was first introduced.

"Many had forgotten all about bacterial dangers like gangrene, *E. coli*, the plague, aspergillus, tetanus, leprosy, animal and bug bites, cholera, dysentery, pneumonia, botulism, meningitis, lyme disease, urinary tract infections, chlamydia, gonorrhea, syphilis, cancroid, and boils. Then there's trichomoniasis, which is actually caused by a parasite, but was successfully treated with antibiotics, and …"

"I get it," El-Auria interrupted.

"Sorry. People were clueless. For the most part, for generations, there had always been a pill they could pop to make it all go away. And, once the permafrost melted shallow graves, many dormant pathogens were released back into the population. Hello again anthrax, Spanish flu, smallpox and, of course, plague.

"The beginning was subtle, but once it started to snowball, things quickly went from bad to worse. Domestic livestock began showing tumors early in their already shortened lifespan. Fish never developed three eyes in the shadow of a power plant but instead died from toxic chemical runoff or heated water released from farms, slaughter houses, manufacturing plants and factories. Waterways became imbalanced and hyper-nutrient due to algae blooms, which caused ox-dep, which, in turn, caused dead zones. Town folk, time and again, woke up to see thousands of dead floating fish.

"Animals raised for human consumption caused diabetes, cancer, heart disease, obesity, lethargy and so many other problems. Those food companies were protected by government agencies and pharmaceutical companies which promoted the treatments of these ailments. Cancer societies were sponsored by entities that sold cancer-causing products and/or their cures. Heart associations were sponsored by cardiovascular disease causing products or their cures. This same idea continues on for diabetes, strokes, high-blood pressure, or arthritis.

"Each of the animal product industries sponsored supposedly 'impartial' education not just for the public, but also for the government and, most shockingly, the medical professionals.

"Everything revolved around making money off of the people; the food industries partnered with the pharmaceutical companies and the government in the cash machine trifecta. The doctors were supposed to help the humans, the drug companies were supposed to help the humans, and the food industry was supposed to help the humans, and the government was supposed to protect humans, but, instead, they banded together *against* the humans.

"Food labeling laws were formed for advertising purposes only, not nutritional. A container of cookies could *legally* be declared sugar-free or fat-free if the serving size was sugar-free or fat-free *or very nearly so*. But that container could actually have measureable sugar and/or fat if there were enough servings. If there were a dozen cookies in that container, the serving size might be one cookie, but despite the gigantic "SUGAR FREE!" label on the packaging, the grams of sugar could quickly add up. Who eats one tiny, thin, diet-sized cookie? The labels were a false sense of security intended to sell products, not protect or educate consumers.

"The humans were victimized and the animals were..." Rachel couldn't finish.

El-Auria waited patiently.

"Agricultural-chemical companies patented their GMO seeds. Three problems immediately occurred. The first is that every crop grown with GMO seeds is sterile, so farmers can't save seeds from last year's crop to plant this year's crop because this would mean a patent infringement. They are completely dependent on that massive conglomerate to reseed. Imagine a smaller nation like Haiti, whose masses had thrived by self-sufficiently reseeding for centuries suddenly needing to buy seeds from some foreign corporation's toll-free phone number to survive because every crop they grew was a one-and-done deal.

"Second, if pollen from a GMO cornfield drifted into a non-GMO cornfield and pollenated even a single stalk, the agricultural company could, and often did, sue that non-GMO farmer because its patent-protected technology was being illegally used by that non-GMO farmer. This action bankrupted small conventional farmers; results that the large companies were more than happy to achieve. If not, then why bother suing a small farm for 'using' their patent when they knew it was accidental and knew that it couldn't be reseeded the following year? If anything, that GMO pollen was *contaminating* someone else's property because they now couldn't sell their products as non-GMO. It should have counted as pollution."

"The third problem was the pesticide-producing, and herbicide-reducing, genetic alterations to the foodstuffs. Although many plants are naturally equipped with pesticides, the GMO manufactured plants have an unnatural high-potency pesticide *intentionally* added to their matrix. This was one of the worst ideas, as it turns out, because more than 100 crop pests became immune to the toxin, some even fed on it, and it was a toxin that consumers couldn't wash off the product to make it safer to eat.

"Many people didn't want to eat foods that were products of GMO, and for most of the world that cared, GMO foods had to be labeled as such, but the United States government refused to do so. It was, however, required to label foods as *organic* (meaning non-GMO, and no herbicides or pesticides were used in the production of the crop), if farmers wanted to sell their produce as organic. In other words, if you don't add anything to this natural product, you have to declare it, but if you mess with it on a genetic level to sterilize it, and to kill bugs with one bite or weeds that should die, but instead grow stronger, then you needn't say a word.

"Even crops like cotton, which is not consumed, was detrimental when artificially enhanced with pest- and weed-killers because of the close-contact textiles have with the body's largest organ; the skin. Cotton was both America's boon and bane, and the irritation and rashes caused by the GMO cotton, along with the massive amounts of water needed to grow the crop, collapsed cotton production in America in favor of hemp. You should see the anti-hemp propaganda and rhetoric that rose up before the death of cotton.

"Anyone who spoke up against this tyranny of GMOs was silenced or over-run by the deep pockets, and the government that should have protected them was, instead, handsomely profiting from it.

"Aside from crops," Rachel caught her breath, "this era's tap water contained any combination of hormones, medications, toxins like lead, viruses, and deadly bacteria.

"Steroids, antibiotics, cholesterol medications, and hormones drastically altered the behavior of sea life, making some reckless, or aggressive. For some it proved to be lethal."

El-Auria said, "That doesn't sound completely correct."

"I'm researching all I can, but there are hundreds of years of historical records in dozens of languages to sort through, and sources to verify. What I'm saying now is, by no means, a final report.

"As for drugs given to animals, you can value them at hundreds of billions of dollars. Just one of those medications, a nonsteroidal anti-inflammatory drug called diclofenac, put three species of vulture on the critically endangered list; they later died out as a direct result. It's surmised that the birds ate meat tainted with the drug, and then this caused kidney-failure in the fowl. Just imagine what all of the other drugs given to food-chain animals must have done."

"Penicillin was discovered in 1928 by Alexander Fleming. He understood, even then, that his 'miracle cure' wouldn't last because of bacteria's natural ability to alter itself to survive the threats of an antibacterial.

"Soon after we began to use them, antibacterial medications entered the water table after being passed through the animal or human body. Animals and humans drank the tainted water and humans ate the tainted animals.

"Each intentional and unintentional consumption of antibiotics compounded the evolution of the bacteria which *naturally* became more resistant to the medication."

After a few moments of quiet, El-Auria urged her to continue, "What happened next?"

"The last useful antibiotic compound was discovered in 1987. Soon after that, it became tragically apparent to most of the medical field that the heyday of this miracle drug was over, while other doctors still prescribed antibiotics for influenza, which it never could cure, and many, if not most patients still stopped using the drug after they were feeling better, which defeated the cure, and actually strengthened the bacteria in their bodies that was making them ill. It was weird."

"Please continue. What is upsetting you so much?"

Rachel grew quiet. Then, thinking to herself, No corn ever grew again after the last sterile stock died. She made an odd, involuntary sound.

"Say again?"

"Since the Age of Agriculture, humans have been genetically modifying their crops to better suit their palate. We looked for the stalks of corncobs that had the fattest, juiciest and most plentiful kernels on them, and we planted those seeds the following season. Then, for the sowing seasons to come, we saved the best kernels from what we had just reaped. We took what suited us best from Nature and disregarded the rest.

"Going even further back in time, we did the same thing to the wolf – our first domesticated animal. We noticed that some wolves were brazen and some were more timid. The fierce animals were killed in defense of our camps, and eventually the more timid and submissive of the pack that came to eat the bones of our dinner were captured and used as protection from the night.

"When they had litters, the wolf pups were culled according to our needs: Those aggressive to humans were killed, and those who tucked their tails and bowed to our demands were spared. When those pups grew up and had litters of their own, those pups were culled too.

"Eventually, early humans had hunting dogs. And, thousands of years later, descendants of those wild, killer wolf packs and their snapping jaws and deep fur coats became bulldogs who couldn't even whelp their own pups because of humanity's need for their standards of size and shape left no room in the bitch's birth canal for the enormous heads of her offspring. Therefore, they had to be surgically removed from her body or she and her pups would die in agony on the day they were supposed to be born.

"Again, we took what suited us best from Nature and disregarded the rest; this is modifying genetics, these are genetically modified organisms. Nature supplied; we decided. Nature naturally genetically modifies, and for thousands of years, humans tended to their crops, their livestock, and their pets, by encouraging traits that Nature provided and they liked, and discontinuing what they didn't. When we looked down on Nature, the wolf became a lapdog. Do you follow?"

"I follow."

"Long after the first domestic cow gave milk to the farmer for his family, or the first seeds of rice were planted to feed a village, humans in the 20th Century set the stage, looked down the eye piece at Nature and said, 'I can do better': GMOs, a new kind of genetically modified organisms, were born.

"As a result, cows in the 21st Century produced four times as much milk as they did in the middle of the previous century. Bigger chicken breasts, more milk, marbled beef, all caused domestic stock to eventually become inedible due to deformities and cancer growths from hormone poisoning, antibiotic resistance, and inbreeding, and crops were sterile and inedible; all due to man's interference with Nature. They changed Nature by tweaking at the chemical level, adding and subtracting. These were no longer Nature's mutations; they were humanity's. This was our legacy."

"That's disgraceful!" El-Auria exclaimed.

"I know. And, that's not even the end of it.

"Humans could have stopped there, but instead they pushed this further.

"When we felt like we got the knack of genetic modifications, and after years of cloning plants and animals, we started to seriously thinking we could do better than Nature with *our own* bodies, *our own* genetics.

"Unlike earlier attempts at ethnic cleansing or the Nazi's love of blond hair and blue eyes, the day arrived when we had children on this Earth who, genetically, had three parental contributors.

"We inserted donor mitochondrial deoxyribonucleic acid (mtDNA), which contains thirty-seven genes, from a healthy ovum and inserted it into the ovum of a woman who has any one of the dozens of mitochondrial-based genetic diseases. Before implanting this altered ovum into the intended birth mother, the new and 'improved' ovum was fertilized by the father's sperm. The new life created carried the genetics of two females and one male – three genetic parents."

"That doesn't sound true," El-Auria declared.

"Once released from the tether of ethics," Rachel continued, "we redoubled our efforts on the search for cures, for cosmetics, for destruction."

El-Auria asked for clarification, "Do you mean weapons?"

"I do. Imagine chemical, biological, radiological as well as plasma weapons research not handicapped by ethics."

"That can't be good," El-Auria stated.

"Blight, dried-up aquafers, locusts, raging storms," Rachel continued. "Seed vaults, banks, and libraries from around the world maintained hundreds-of-thousands of seeds and their genetic lines for protection in cases of crop destruction up to, and including, nuclear or world war. But, when the time came for their use, they nearly failed because there was hardly any untainted soil, non-toxic water, or clean air in which to germinate these precious life-lines. The once-fertile Earth was impoverished, toxic, or flat-out sterilized by the hand of man."

"This all rather tangled, but if I understand you correctly, it *is* disturbing."

"We were Earth's necrotizing *fasciitis*. Humans had to keep lopping off huge tracts of land and water ways as we destroyed it beyond repair. 'Cancer Villages' became 'Cancer Cities.' Sure, Nature would eventually return, if given proper a span of time, but whatever was there before the humans, lived there with the humans, as well as the humans themselves, were never to return."

"Why? Did any of your research explain why they did all of this?"

Rachel looked at El-Auria, "Because we could."

"Disturbing, indeed."

"There were body farms, but instead of the traditional dead bodies donated for scientific research and displayed in controlled outdoor experiments, 'body farming' took on a whole new meaning. We had warehouses full of horror-movie human-pig hybrids growing organs for those who could afford it, and other horrors followed even that."

"If I could vomit, I would."

"Indeed. I just might vomit enough for both of us. If we were to personify what we did to Mother Nature, it would have to be something akin to a testosterone-fueled rampage of power, strength, force, alpha-male domination, and gratification of our needs over the needs of anything else in the world."

"That seems appropriate."

"Our world became the view from the outhouse toilet. We were sitting on a pile of shit looking up through a hole in the wall to see the beautiful stars above."

"Enough said."

CHAPTER 17

"APRÈS NOUS, LE DELUGE!"

"Why didn't they know that this would happen?"

Hadley replied absently, "They did know."

"That's horseshit. If they knew that this would happen, but did it anyway, then that means that the destruction was *intentional*. Disasters are inevitable, but tragedies are avoidable. This whole mess was completely avoidable!"

"You are correct."

"But, WHY?!" Sagan demanded.

Hadley wanted to put this conversation to rest, "It would appear that all that mattered to those empowered to make the decisions was that they were solving the problems in front of them without the worry of what happens in the future as a result of their choices. It's a typical human behavior, particularly if money was to be made, or in danger of being lost."

"Plastics and nuclear power: We wanted it, we invented it, we manufactured it, we sold it, we grabbed it, we used it, we failed it, and we left it for later generations to deal with, long after we stopped using it," Sagan exclaimed.

"We were fooling ourselves into thinking we could handle nuclear power or its pollution," Sagan was just getting warmed up.

"Sagan..."

"The highly radioactive waste needed to be stored safely for hundreds of thousands of years, but nothing humans could ever create would last that long and the engineers knew that, even back then. So, they created safe storage for 700,000 tons of untouchable death knowing full-well that it would only last long enough for a generation other than their own would have to address the dangerous situation of leaking casks. And generations later, again."

"Sagan…"

"Even after nuclear power was discontinued due to its extremely hazardous waste, generations had to face contamination and destruction from ever-faulting storage of radioactive death. And, that's just the waste that was legally and ethically disposed.

"Any contact with radioactive runoff *permanently* altered the genetics of any living entity as well as their progeny for as long as that genetic line existed.

"Think about it. Every eighteen months, in every power plant, nuclear fuel rods were considered spent, and were replaced. The spent fuel rods were too hot to move out of the facility at this point, so they went into cooling tanks for about ten years. No rush.

"Because of this accumulation, there was far more nuclear power in these on-site waste pools than there was actually currently in use in the reactors. The waste was also hotter spent, temperature-wise, than it was new, with each rod at about 3000 degrees Fahrenheit.

"Now, multiply the 18 months by over 500 nuclear reactor facilities and sites by, say, 20 years of production. The x-factor here is how many fuel rods were used per cycle, but let's say 10. That's almost 2 million spent fuel rods, using the low-end of each variable! There is so much accumulated nuclear waste that it could have powered the entire *world* for a century!

"Remember the on-site spent fuel rod pools? Those are actually cooling towers using something known as heavy water – forty feet of heavy water. If that water is lowered, or if those spent fuel rods are exposed for any reason, these fuel rods *explode*. And, when that happens, everything in the vicinity and down-wind *dies*.

"These dead zones are as dangerous as Picher, Oklahoma, as unlivable as Centralia, Pennsylvania, and as inhospitable as San Francisco's Hunters Point in California. Around the world, dead towns became dead areas, and dead areas with their associated waterways and windward ways, had to be amputated from human history.

"Those fuel rods have to be protected for thousands of years. That heavy water has to be protected for thousands of years. Boots, gloves, machinery, entire facilities, Madam Curie's notebooks, have to be protected for thousands of years. Plants would come back, as would the animal life, but they didn't know the dangers.

"You could shoot nuclear waste into space and hope that the craft doesn't malfunction and explode on the launch pad or in the atmosphere. Oh, and you'd need enough money to build a fleet of crafts that could push itself plus hundreds-of-thousands of tons of radioactive payload into the heavens. You also would need fuel to power the crafts. And, you would need some entity or country to take responsibility for this task, pay for it, build it and launch it over and over again for a century, and still barely make a dent in the stockpiles. Or, you could drop hermetically sealed encasements of radioactive waste into the deepest parts of the ocean, and then just sail away. But then, after your generation passed, the encasements would become fragile with time, irretrievable in their depth, and someone else's problem."

Hadley tried to get Sagan's attention, "Hey!"

But Sagan persisted, "What about wind energy, solar power, hydropower, hydrolysis power, algae, viruses, wave energy, geothermal, perpetual motion, ion drives, anti-matter..?"

"There was a negative pushback on climate change," Hadley said. "Even high-ranking people believed, or chose to believe, that the facts put forth to them by scientists were lies. This led to a dramatic drop in funding for research and development of alternative fuels.

"Coupled with this," Hadley continued, "the baseload of power increased beyond what even fossil fuels could maintain.

"It was soon after this realization that another one hit: Any alternative source of power proved to be too weak, technologically speaking, to feed the power-hungry masses," Hadley stated succinctly.

"Solar power had the best chance; it really could have made the difference, but there were too many people wanting too much power for any delicate network of solar-powered grids to take hold and flourish into more networks and more power: Anything less was inconvenient."

Hadley watched Sagan's face fall, but continued, "Every other chance to overcome fossil fuels failed because humanity couldn't curb the hunger, couldn't overcome the addiction, for more power. And these fossil fuels had a long list of horrible consequences; most notably, it was the dominant contributor to climate change, carrying more than fifty percent of the blame. Nuclear energy was the only option left."

Sagan's head shook in disbelief.

Hadley felt that this conversation had come to a close.

"And, what about plastics?!"

"Sagan…"

"Twenty trillion tons of plastic have been produced since it was invented in the 1950s! We couldn't reverse its reign of terror for the life of us, or for the lives of trillions of other creatures. An archeological dig, millions of years from now would be interesting." Sagan assumed a scholarly tone, "… There's the boundary clearly recording the meteor-hit. Its black strata can be seen in any dig anywhere in the world. And, can you see this thin line here? That's a layer of hydrocarbons from the Era of Plastics. They thought they were brilliant, but their cheaper-faster-lighter-disposable economy created so much unrecycled plastic that even our water now contains, in its matrix, plastic molecules. The type of sedimentary rock you see here is classified as plastiglomerate. There are billions and billi-"

Hadley feigned interest, "Fascinating!"

"Really?"

"No."

"This didn't have to happen, Hadley!"

"I know, my friend."

"But, didn't they know about hemp? It literally grows as fast and as easily as a weed. It's biodegradable and naturally pest-resistant. It could have replaced more than 50,000 different commercially sold products like wood, paper, plastics, and anything cotton. It's even an edible protein!"

Hadley said again, "I know. But if it had evolved to become as big as it could have, then what would have happened to all of those other industries?"

"Are you serious? We didn't need wood pulp for toilet paper! We didn't need to use so much water and chemicals to raise bug-free, weed-free cotton crops. We didn't need to add to the plastic choking wildlife and floating in our oceans. Hemp plants have even been used to absorb nuclear waste in soil! Did you know that?!"

"I know, my friend," Hadley repeated softly.

"Who…what… WHY?!" Sagan was near apoplectic.

"Après nous, le deluge!"

CHAPTER 18

NEO-HUMANITY

In this other world, the liberty and freedom of "Religion said I could do it," was as arbitrary as the constraint and hindrance of, "Religion said I couldn't do it," because you could have been born into any religion, and if born into another religion you would be for something that you're now against, or against something that you're now for. You could also convert to another religion or even leave religion completely.

This other world's religions peaked and then destroyed themselves, imploding after they became more and more exclusive rather than inclusive of other people and other faiths.

"God loves you, but we don't because you…"

"We love you, but…"

"You could worship here, but you're a…"

"We don't want…"

"We don't permit…"

"We don't like…"

These early religions were rich with hundreds of billions of dollars but, oddly, promoted poverty; they were led by men, but decreed what could be done to a woman's body; preached forgiveness of sin, but excommunicated sinners; and they, time and again, considered their dominion over the Earth, their God-given right.

Xenophanes of Colophon once thought that if horses could draw, their gods would look like horses. That is to say, humanity created gods in their own image. If cannibals had gods, then their gods would be cannibals and therefore their behaviors, no matter how bizarre or prohibited by others, would be completely normal and acceptable by the cannibals.

As R.G. Ingersoll once said, "In nature there are neither rewards nor punishments; there are consequences." After thousands upon thousands of gods roamed the hearts and minds of humanity, this other world's neo-humanity was much more latitudinarian with their neighbor's faiths than previous generations and eventually simplified their religion to just three inclusive entities: Mother Nature, Father Time, and the Universe.

In this other world, they didn't believe that life was naturally balanced and that they spent their lives trying to maintain that narrow corridor of perfect equilibrium.

Instead, they believed that they, being a part of Nature, were inherently unbalanced and messy and they spent their lives trying to achieve a peaceful, generous, and loving balance with those equally messy creatures around them.

They weren't intolerant of others who weren't perfect; they were kind to them because, they too, were living in the chaos.

CHAPTER 19

COUPLING

In this other world, because it was the woman's body that created the baby after conception, gave birth, and nursed, it was the woman's choice to mate with any available man or not at all. This held true even if infertile, menstruating, already pregnant or menopausal. And, because the father of the child could be in another settlement or even on another continent, the baby was raised by her and carried-on, if she wished it, her name.

If a man didn't want to mate with a woman, he declared himself unavailable.

The mating rituals of neo-humanity were ephemeral. Family groups were more like loosely constructed clans with many children, sub-adults, adults, and the supraquadragenarian elderly; strictly speaking, there were no legal ties.

Heterosexuality was never presumed; homosexuality was never forbidden. One's sexual identity and preference were displayed without shame or dishonor. Nudity was rare but by no means taboo or shocking to witness, even by children.

A breastfeeding woman was honored and if she happened to be in public, passersby would speak in hushed tones so as not to disturb the baby. As voices dropped off, a respectful nod was given to the mother and she returned it in kind as a token of gratitude for their deference to her sleepy child. Once away from the family, conversation returned to a normal level and people would go about their business.

So many previous social constructs didn't interest neo-humanity. One could still be the man of the household while making breakfast for one's family, or sewing a patch on a kid's pants.

In all-male societies of the past, like on-board most military ships of the world, men prepared the meals and cleaned-up the messes of others, men did the laundry and ironing, and men scoured, cleaned and polished every inch of the vessel. Men even tended to the sick and wounded under the guidance of the ship's doctor; they were *nursing* when they change bedpans, cleaned-up puke and washed bodies. They were *military!* They weren't weaker humans for doing their duty, their share; they were stronger, and they made their team of shipmates stronger and their ships ran flawlessly if they did their duty, and dangerously substandard if they didn't.

Women used to have to go through extraordinary steps to secure an education in a man's world. In fact, the first woman of Great Britain to be awarded a doctorate in medicine earned it while being disguised as a man. Born Margaret Ann Bulkley, she was the first to successfully perform a cesarean in South Africa, and while other doctors were still bleeding people to make them better, James Barry, as she was known, insisted on cleanliness, fresh air, and good food. She practiced medicine for fifty years as a man, and rose in the ranks of the British Army, eventually becoming the Medical Inspector. Only after her death in 1865, was it discovered that the venerable Dr. James Barry was a woman. This proved to be a deep embarrassment for the British Army, and all records regarding their renowned surgeon who served for more than forty years, were sealed for over a century.

It didn't have to be this way, so changes were made. It was finally understood by later generations that one cannot adapt with such ridged definitions, and if one does not adapt, one dies. Many walls came down; much anger was lost.

Women could be mountain climbers, chess-masters, oil rig workers, investigators, prosecutors, pirates, generals and world leaders; men didn't have to carry the load by themselves because of perceived hypermasculinity.

Men could obey the orders of women; women could obey the orders of men.

Women could be doctors; men could be nurses.

Men could be professional dancers; women could be professional fighters.

Women could be expert card players; men could be married to politicians.

Men could knit, crotchet, latch-hook, cross-stitch, sew, quilt, embroider, needle-point, and weave; women could be mechanics, welders, miners, and assembly line supervisors.

Women could be sexually aggressive; men could be virgins.

Men could be florists or flautists; women could be wheelwrights or wrestlers.

Men could cook; women could fish.

Women could be superheroes without nipples piercing their clothes, showing cleavage, or bending over; men could faint.

Men could wear jewelry; women could have tattoos.

Men could be office assistants; women could hunt and farm.

Men could have long hair, wear wigs, and hairpieces; women could have bald heads.

Women could serve their country; men could clean house.

Men could chose to never have children or even chose to never marry; women could make those same choices.

A man changing his baby's diaper is no more a "Super Dad" than a woman doing the same thing could be called a "Super Mom." And man doesn't "baby sit" his own children any more than their mother does.

Women don't have to produce babies. They could produce plays, or television shows or movies. They could direct them, too! They don't have to smile, stay quiet, and be invisible.

A strong woman doesn't mean that there is a weak man.

People had been sewing clothes using a needle for 50,000 years, yet the t-shirt had to be invented in the 20th Century because bachelors couldn't sew on a replacement button. Caring for the family is not a lesser thing. It's not something that is shameful or "below" any human being. It's not something that a man has to delegate to a second-class citizen or servant; he can do it himself with the same amount of effort as, and as shameless as, a woman. And, because a woman is the Chief Executive Officer of a company that does not mean that her husband has to make sure dinner is on her table. It's choice for both sexes.

It's opportunity for both sexes.

Finally, neo-humanity was working together.

CHAPTER 20

FINISTERRE

The cornerstone was set.

Then, on a historic day, and with much fanfare, humans traveled into space once again. Like India pulling the Aryabhata on an ox cart through the dusty streets of its third-world economy, neo-humanity returned to the sky.

Ambassadors, town elders, and teachers from near and far flocked to witness the next big step in their reach for the stars before returning to their homes with stories to tell one and all.

The festival went on for days. After feasting and story-telling, games were played, arts and crafts were taught, goods and supplies were traded.

Because so much had been learned from museums, at these festivals, loom and pottery, sailing and saddlery, agriculture, technology, languages, environmental studies, forestry, history, medicine, meditation, mathematics, music, sociology, public health, resource conservation, wildlife biology, animal husbandry, ecosystem management, geosciences, engineering, cosmology and other specialties were taught, and new friends and families were made.

Preparations were in place; it was time to ascend to the space station known as the *Oasis* and bring the legendary sleeping astronaut back home.

Finally, Feis was rescued and welcomed by all, only to become the new Typhoid Mary, infecting the tender population that had no resistance or treatment for this bacterium.

In less than a year, typhoid fever decimated humankind, and not long after that, it completely eradicated them.

Even if there were carriers that didn't get sick, the survivors were too few and far between. Once again, Feis became the sole survivor as the world's population completely succumbed to this extinction-level event.

For lack of better harbinger imagery, Nyx had arrived to usher human beings into the darkness of their downfall. The faint, soft, helpless cries of millions of fevered people were witnessed by no one but themselves.

All countries went dark but for a mere handful of lights that represented a single human being in fifteen or so isolated locations around the world. They wrote in a journal, talked to the dead, or looked to the stars, each believing that they were the last person alive on Earth. Then, all but one light flickered out.

In this other world, Yossarian, the last human alive on Earth, knew that humanity could have survived the repeated occurrences of population bottlenecking had they lived together in higher populations. But, of course, if they had lived together in higher populations, there would have been a major increase in disagreement, in dissension, in disease, and in death – each of which would have decreased the populace in its own special way causing an otherwise healthy people to die before their time.

The one who could solve this died of that... And, the one who could solve that died of this. Humanity simply could not adapt to changing conditions, and their time to figure out the proper balance to ensure survival had run out, just as it had for every extinct organism that had ever lived. Every time. Everywhere.

With that final thought, Yossarian's unseeing eyes closed one last time. And, with a whimper, this world ended.

~ ~ ~

A day, a century, or a thousand years later, aliens arrive. They became desperately sick and all died, except for a sole survivor who was able to escape Planet Earth and head home...

END

PART III

A PRIORI

CHAPTER 21

CONTAGION TO THIS WORLD

At the same time, in another Universe there is another Earth, and on this Earth, decisions were made. We…

Another world is not only possible, she is on her way.
On a quiet day, I can hear her breathing.
(Arundhati Roy)

Points to Be Made

Q: Why did you write this book?

A: I became disenchanted with dystopian science-fiction; it seemed to be fear-driven and all about guns, violence, power, and force. Utopian stories were more interesting, because there was always a chink in the perfection, but the settings were far too unrealistic and unattainable for my taste.

What if we were *naturally* non-violent in the future, and not ruled by hate, envy, greed, aggression, and dominance? What if we, far into the future, had to live with the mistakes we are currently making in this modern age? What if we had the same incidences, but made different choices? Only parallel universes could give me the option of restarting society, again and again. If I were to write a sequel, the book would be called *The Darkness of Their Downfall*, and it would start right where *Contagion to this World* left off.

I wanted this story to be comprehensive of all that has been contaminated: It's all connected. You cannot save the blue whale, and be done with it, because shark fin soup is still favored in Hong Kong restaurants. You cannot save the rainforest, and be done with it, because that won't ween humanity off of fossil fuels. And, the pervasive attitude of dominance with the rules of Patriarchy has proven to be a destructive force on humanity and Earth. If this was altered, but it took devastating wars to accomplish this feat then, again, we've lost.

Q: How much research did you do?

A: I could state hundreds of sources, but for as many as I have, this would start looking more like a research paper. For current news, I rely on USA Today, the Associated Press, and other reputable sources. I also love Top Ten lists like TopTenz.net, and sources of random facts like RefDesk.com, FactSlides.com, and FactRetreiver.com. And, let's not forget the internet; I can query anything, at any time, for any reason.

Also, I'm married to a former submariner, so I've grilled him about life aboard a water-tight U.S. Navy boat, and then altered that information to serve as my space station.

I have researched aquaponics, bees, and fish. I'm not 100% sure bees could live as my hive has because, as I understand it, they are usually flower-specific, but that's ok, because where facts leave off, fiction takes over. Case-in-point, blue tilapia exists and can be used just as my fish have, but I needed something that could be easily sexed and separated, so I created orange tilapia (where the females look different than the males) for my story.

Q: In this book, you speak of superbugs and the "inevitable" end of the efficacy of antibiotics. Are these true?
A: Yes. In many ways, we are already there.

Q: Why are there so many lists and repetitive sentences?
A: I could have simplified and boiled a subject down to a single sentence, but so much pain and agony would have been glossed over and quickly forgotten. Those, I instead felt, needed to be driven home. The last word I added to the brainstorming of the worst words in the human language was *incest*. To some, it's just a word, but to millions of others it's their grief, their life, their suffering. How could I have possibly left that out?

As it stands now, I have undoubtedly missed something in this or another chapter. That (or those) omission(s) were not intentional. It took months of collating these horrors. For many, I scribbled in the dark after waking in the middle of the night. I finally put "Book Notes" on each 5x7 yellow note pad (by the bed, by the bathtub, by my chair, and in my purse), so that if I never woke up again, my last (misunderstood) words weren't, "baby-raping."

In my opinion, each of these acts against humanity, animals, and the Earth, needs even more attention than I've given them here. They don't deserve to be merely added to a list that some fussy reader might gripe about being too long, or left off of a list for the very same reason. They deserve paragraphs, or even chapters in this book. What you have read is my own compromise. I urge you to read those chapters again, and think about the enormity and history of each and every word. Don't think about how they don't affect you because they don't apply to you; think about how *hundreds of billions of other people, and trillions of plants and animals, and Earth itself,* are affected outside of your tiny (no disrespect intended) realm of being. You might find that they do affect you after all.

Q: Why are names so important in this story?

A: The names are important because they each have their own backstory. I don't have to say that Dr. Snoopy Doghouse's parents named him after an ancient cartoon dog from long ago, I can just say his name. From there, one of two things will happen. Either you know who Snoopy is, and are instantly fully aware of the significance of the name, or you research the name and are then fully aware of the significance. Either way, I feel it adds depth to a character and to that character's motivation in a story like this.

Early in my writing I told my husband I had no idea what to name my space agency, so he asked, "What's your favorite planet?" "Saturn, of course," I replied. When I looked it up, the "Saturn Space Agency" became the "Saturnian Space Agency," because, for one, they weren't going to Saturn, and two, the reign of the god Saturn was referred to as the "golden age," and "Saturnian days" refers to a prosperous, peaceful and happy time. Altogether, my space agency was at the top of its game, and cruising along like a well-oiled machine.

Dr. Feis' name was the first one I chose for a historical reference. I took "FEIS" from *Final Environmental Impact Statement* in U.S. governmental reports. This one was from a nuclear report about where to safely store nuclear waste. Wow, were they wrong.

Dr. Uluru Kata-Tjuta's is named after a rock formation in Australia. Uluru is the aboriginal name for a massive monolith deemed to be the largest rock in the world, and Kata Tjuta (no hyphen) is a sister rock in the same grouping. This little fragile man is named after an immense rock formation.

Themyscira is Wonder Woman's home world. Kintsukuroi is a Japanese term that means, "To repair with gold." It is understood that pottery mended with gold is far more valuable and more beautiful for having been broken. Once you understand those names, the chapter has deeper meaning.

As for the chapter title, Derecho, it was described to me as a straight-lined, inland hurricane. I felt that this described all of the women of the world who were, and still are, legally relegated to the indoors. The only way to stop any atmospheric storm, even a powerhouse derecho, is equality. To reach human equality, there's only one direction to go.

No need to look for historical references for the names Zander, Zoe, Marcus, Kristy, and Travis; they are names close to my heart.

Q: Why so much Latin?
A: Latin phrases, (or French, or a Frenchman using Latin), are succinct. They can clarify a point or add a specific emotion to an argument. *Castigat ridendo mores* was Jean de Santeul's way of using satirical writing to promote social change. His idea was to address and change laws by pointing out how absurd they were, just as I am doing here. *Castigat ridendo mores* is Latin for "laughter corrects customs."

Q: Why are Chapters 10 and 11 so long; couldn't it have been summed-up?
A: Ah, yes, Hesiod's lecture on Patriarchal Laws. All of those laws had to be stated. Leaving just one out would erase the Patriarchal oppression of, at the very least, thousands of people. This being said, I have no doubt that I have left so many out, that they must number in the hundreds.

Patriarchal societies are not universal; it is merely something that we keep reinforcing. Do you know why it's said that we *testify* in court?

The word "testify" originates from the word *testicle*. It's from a time in Rome when men would grab their crotch and swear on their testicles that they were telling the truth.

In this story, Hesiod says, "One noted philosopher even saw women as a different species!" That noted philosopher was the historical Hesiod himself.

Q: What's your inspiration?

A: I love science, science-fiction, and documentaries, like Charles Darwin's *On the Origin of Species by Means of Natural Selection* (1859); H. G. Wells' *Time Machine* (1895); Ayn Rand's *Anthem* (1938); Rachel Carson's *Under the Sea Wind* (1941), *The Sea Around Us* (1951), *The Edge of the Sea* (1955), *Silent Spring* (1962); Ray Bradbury's *The Martian Chronicles* (1950); Isaac Asimov's *Foundation* series (1951); Richard Matheson's *I Am Legend* (1954); Arthur C. Clarke's *Space Odyssey* series (1968); *Soylent Green* (1973); Richard P. Feynman's *Surely You're Joking, Mr. Feynman!* (1985); Stephen Hawking's *A Brief History of Time* (1988), and *The Universe in a Nutshell* (2001); Bill Nye the Bow Tie Guy (I jest with love); BBC Earth; 30-plus (that I've witnessed) years of David Attenborough's work including *Life, Blue Planet* and my absolute favorite, *Rise of the Animals: Triumph of the Vertebrates; Contact* (1997); Lucy Lawless' *Warrior Women* (2003); Michio Kaku's *Parallel Worlds* (2004); Sigourney Weaver's *Planet Earth* (2006); *A Long Way Gone: Memoirs of a Boy Soldier* (2007); *The Future of Water* (2007); *Food, Inc.* (2008); Stephen Fry's *Last Chance to See* (2009); History Channel's *Life After People* (2009); *I Am Nujood, Age 10 and Divorced* (2010); *Fat, Sick, & Nearly Dead* (2010); *Frozen Planet* (2011); *Vegucated* (2011); *The Bay* (2012); *Chasing Ice* (2012); Neil deGrasse Tyson's *The Inexplicable Universe: Unsolved Mysteries* (The Great Courses, 2012) and *Cosmos: A Spacetime Odyssey* (2014); *Blackfish* (2013); *I Am Malala* (2013); *Life Below Zero* (2013); *The Out List* (2013); *Changing Seas* (2014); Dr. Sylvia Earle's *Mission Blue* (2014); *American Experience: The Blackout* (2015); Dr. Amanda Foreman's fantastic *Ascent of Woman* (2015); *Consumed* (2015); PBS' *In Defense of Food* (2015) and *9 Months That Made You* (2016); Vanessa

Paradis' *Terra* (2015); *A Plastic Ocean* (2016); Jim al-Khalili's *The Beginning and End of the Universe* (2016); *Blood on the Mountain* (2016); *Minimalism* (2016); *Daughters of Destiny* (2017); *Losing Sight of the Shore* (2017); *What the Health* (2017); TED conferences; and of course, *Firefly* (2002), and *The Big Bang Theory* (2007)!

My questions for you:

Q: How did you picture the Director is Chapter 3? My character writing style is minimalist.

For main characters, I do not describe them physically, or state where they come from or where they went to school, etc. This is so the reader can imagine them with their own ethnicity, age, and background.

For secondary characters, as often as I can, I do not even define their sex, but just identify their titles, "the Director."

I do this so that the reader's imagination can fill in the blanks, and this happens automatically. If I said that the director's name was Joe Heavyweight and he was six-feet-six inches tall, had gap teeth, pale skin, brown hair, brown eyes, and wore a red Harvard sweatshirt to the gym every day, then no one would ever see the Director as a woman, Asian, African, Middle-Eastern, educated elsewhere, sickly, slight, or short.

Q: How did you picture Dr. Feis or Hadley? Or, the Interviewer, the Environmentalist, and the Producer? How did you imagine the camera operator? Was Hesiod male, like the character's namesake?

Many of the characters were not physically described in this book. Were Hadley or El-Auria even human? It's entirely up to your imagination.

Q: What do the aliens in this story look like? I didn't create them, you did. And the characters you created in your own mind are like no one else's in the world even though you were all reading the same book.

Edmund Wilson said, "No two persons ever read the same book." I feel I've taken this idea a step further.

~ ~ ~

Finally, I'd like to say that I am an amateur human being. I crave knowledge and absorb knowledge, but I cannot always accurately represent my knowledge on paper, and I am far less correct when trying to achieve such a feat verbally.

But, my outward limitations will not keep me from learning inward, if that makes any sense; I hotly pursue education. Adding to that, my imagination is famished; it is constantly seeking succor. To attend to these two feverish demands, my nightstand has held books ranging from Sylvia Plath to J.K. Rowling, Agatha Christie to Nelson DeMille, Rachel Carson to Dian Fossey, Homer and Shakespeare to Gabriel García Márquez, James Herriot to Alison Weir, Thomas Keneally to Malala Yousafzai, Pearl S. Buck to Richard Wright, Melville to Doyle, Madeleine L'Engle to Scott O'Dell, Bill Watterson to Douglas Adams, and Stephen King to Stephen Hawking.

To me, these are all brave new worlds. Oh, and Aldous Huxley!

- ad altiora tendo -

www.Facebook.com/ContagionToThisWorld
www.Facebook.com/LandfillMiners
www.LandfillMiners.com

Other books by this author:
Mediocre – Making Fun of Life
Pen to Paper – Making Fun of Life

www.Facebook.com/MakingFunofLife

Made in the USA
Coppell, TX
31 January 2020

15204581R00088